FLEMBER

THE SECRET BOOK

WWW   www.davidficklingbooks.com

JAMIE SMART'S

FLEMBER

THE SECRET BOOK

David Fickling Books

31 Beaumont Street
Oxford OX1 2NP, UK

Flember: The Secret Book
is a
DAVID FICKLING BOOK

First published in Great Britain in 2019 by
David Fickling Books,
31 Beaumont Street,
Oxford, OX1 2NP

Text & Illustrations © Jamie Smart, 2019

978-1-910989-46-3

1 3 5 7 9 10 8 6 4 2

The right of Jamie Smart to be identified as the author and
illustrator of this work has been asserted in accordance
with the Copyright, Designs and Patents Act 1988.

Papers used by David Fickling Books are from
well-managed forests and other responsible sources.

MIX
Paper from
responsible sources
FSC® C018072

DAVID FICKLING BOOKS Reg. No. 8340307

A CIP catalogue record for this book is available from the British Library.
Printed and bound in Great Britain by Clays Ltd, Elcograf S.p.A.

whatever holds your heart together

An Introduction

There is an island.
It lies just over the horizon.
Always, just over the horizon.

Except, that is, for the unlucky few who chance upon it, those who sail off course and sail too close. Their ships tear like paper against the huge jagged rocks of the coastline. Dark, swirling oceans drag them under, pick at their bones and then spit out their remains across the poisonous black sand of the beaches.

This island, *Flember Island*, has secrets it does not want to give up.

1
The Village of Eden, in the Mountains

Nestled upon Flember Island's southern most mountain, like a beacon of light in the darkness, was the small village of Eden. And whilst Eden might have looked scary from the outside – being, as it was, concealed behind a ten-metre-high wall of sharpened tree trunks – on the inside *flember*, the energy of life, thrived. Forests bustled, meadows swayed, ponds glistened. Waterfalls crashed. Rivers trickled.

Villagers ambled about in the morning sunshine.

Our story starts here, in Eden, but away from the orange and blue rooftops of the streets. Down a winding path, across a crumbling stone bridge, in a clearing before Spindletree Forest.

Where a small house was to be found.

Around the back of the house was a workshop, hanging dangerously over the edge of a cliff. Alongside it a series of rickety wooden platforms had been stacked. They swayed to the left or to the right, depending which way the breeze was blowing. And there, standing on the highest platform, was a boy called Dev.

He had sparkling, inquisitive, emerald-green eyes. A faint wash of freckles across his nose. A tumble of messy hair wedged beneath his cat-eared helmet. He wore a black vest, backpack, chunky blue boots and a long orange scarf, which fluttered out behind him like a writhing fibbler eel.

BOILK. His stomach lurched.

Were he to fall from this height, he'd fall for ages. Bouncing against the steep cliff face all the way down into Percy's Scrapyard. Probably landing on some deeply uncomfortable sticky-out thing.

A cold sweat prickled out from his skin. He closed his eyes. Deep breath. All thoughts of falling forced from his mind.

Everything fell calm.

Everything was silent.

Only the quiet ruffling of his wing feathers.

And then, the shouting started.

'WINGS?'

Calm, remember? Caaaalm.

'Dev, I know you can hear me! You're wearing WINGS?'

Dev readjusted the harness around his shoulders. 'I plucked a lot of chickens to make these! They're perfectly safe, Mum!'

He opened one eye. There, on the workshop balcony below, stood his mother. Dressed all in green, from her boots to her helmet. Glaring up at Dev through a few stray ringlets of red hair.

'The RAMP, though!' She pointed to the boards and panels sloping down from the top platform. 'What's *that* for?'

'It curves up at the perfect angle to propel me into the sky!' Dev replied. 'To fly among the flemberbugs!'

6

His mother stared at him in disbelief. 'FLY?'

Dev pointed at a tiny dot fluttering across the sky. 'THERE!' he exclaimed, lifting a glass jar from his belt and watching the dot pass behind it. 'The first flemberbug of the season! I want to study it!'

Her face fell into a stern frown. 'This is NOT one of your better ideas, Dev. No one ever flew with chicken-feather wings. Even the chickens struggle to.'

'Oh! I'm not just using the wings.' Dev grinned, clipping the jar to his belt. 'I've also invented . . . CHEESE BOOTS!'

He pointed down to his boots. Around the heel of each was a small round canister, and inside, an unpleasant looking splodge of white unpasteurised cheese.

'The Cheese Emporium's finest.' Dev beamed. 'Or worst, depending on how you look at it. The yeasts in cheese are fascinating, Mum. Did you know, if you let cheese rot for long enough, it gives off an almighty blast of energy? Enough, I worked out, to send me

INVENTION 495: Chicken Wings
INVENTION 496: Cheese Boots

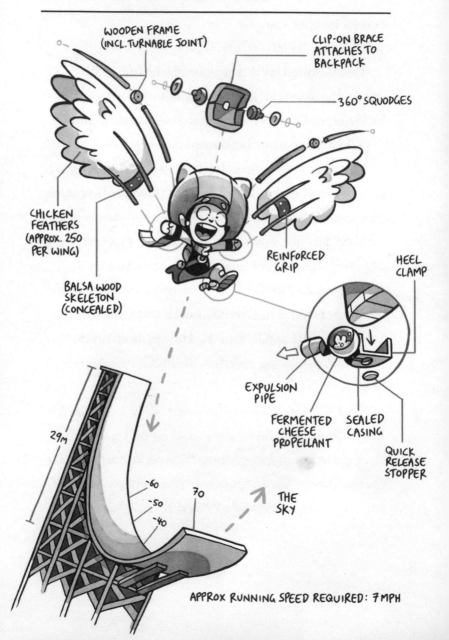

WOODEN FRAME
(INCL. TURNABLE JOINT)

CLIP-ON BRACE
ATTACHES TO
BACKPACK

360° SQUODGES

CHICKEN
FEATHERS
(APPROX. 250
PER WING)

REINFORCED
GRIP

HEEL
CLAMP

BALSA WOOD
SKELETON
(CONCEALED)

EXPULSION
PIPE

FERMENTED
CHEESE
PROPELLANT

SEALED
CASING

QUICK
RELEASE
STOPPER

29m

-60
-50
-40

70

THE
SKY

APPROX RUNNING SPEED REQUIRED: 7 MPH

flying . . .'

'Dev, this is DANGEROUS!'

'I KNOW!' Dev's stomach *BOILKED* again. 'I'm only sixty-three per cent sure it'll work.'

He closed both eyes, gulped and readied himself.

'I'll let you know if it doesn't!'

His hands slid into the harness straps, flapping out his long, white, fluffy wings to their full extent. His mother shouted something, but it was lost to the breeze – Dev leapt from the top platform and *CLOMP CLOMPED* loudly down the ramp.

'Now, Cheese Boots,' he whispered under his breath, stamping his heels on each step.

BOILK! BLURK! BRPPT! The boots spluttered.

'NOW, CHEESE BOOTS, NOW!'

BLRPPPTTT!

'NOW, NOW, NOWWW!'

But it was too late.

A sense of intense regret crackled through his veins as the ramp disappeared from beneath his feet, and Dev P. Everdew was in the air.

And he was screaming.

And then squealing with laughter.

'I'm FLYING!' he yelled, tilting his wings to catch the wind. Every breeze yanked him higher into the sky, knocking a little more breath from his lungs. Tears spilled down his cheeks. His heart felt like it was going to burst from his chest.

It was utterly,
utterly
wonderful.

He watched his shadow roll across the towering chimneys of Percy's Scrapyard. A small figure scrambled between the rusting metal hills, splashing through the shiny black puddles. Even from up here Dev could tell who it was.

White helmet, bunches of bright blue hair spilling out from either side.

Small.

But *fast*.

'I can see you, Dev!' the young girl yelled, lifting a pair of goggles from her eyes. 'Dev, can you see me?'

'Mina! Do you like my wings?' Dev replied. 'They're made from chickens!'

'I can't hear you!' Mina produced her favourite red teddy bear, and waved it above her head. 'You're too high up!'

'I think I'm too high up!' Dev

laughed. 'I can't hear you!'

'Can you hear me though?' Mina reached the scrapyard gates, and excitedly jumped up and down on the spot.

Dev tilted again, rising higher, until soon he was gliding above the rooftops of Middle Eden. He breathed in the deliciously sweet smells from Rousseau's Bakery, the delicate fragrance of Agatha Bloom's Floral Adore-All, before gagging at the pong from Rosa Mildew's Cheese Emporium.

A small group of children followed his shadow. They wore a variety of random objects as helmets, and one even had a cape that flapped behind him as

he ran.

'Space Fleet!' Dev shouted. 'Think I can make it to the moon?'

Space Fleet's commander, a small boy named Sam, raised his fists in the air.

'I bet you can, Lieutenant Dev!' he yelled from inside his slightly-too-large helmet. 'And you'll bring us back an alien!'

The other three children running alongside all cheered, until one by one they were grabbed by their parents and hustled back indoors.

'Well, I'll try,' Dev chuckled. 'If it'll fit inside my jar.'

'We ain't following if you go over!' a stern voice shouted up.

A number of angry-looking men in uniform spilled onto the path, their helmets clonking together as they ran, their thin swords waving in the air.

'The WALL!' another shouted.

'You're about to go over The WALL!'

And then there it was, erupting up from a thick tangle of brambles. *The Wall.* A huge towering barricade of tree trunks, their tips sharpened to a point, as tall as two houses stacked on top of each other.

Whatever else lived on this island, The Wall looked sturdy enough to keep it out.

'The flemberbug!' Dev gasped, suddenly remembering why he was up here. 'I only wanted . . . the . . . flemberbug!'

He slammed his foot against the tip of The Wall and pushed himself back towards the village. And then he could see it again – that little

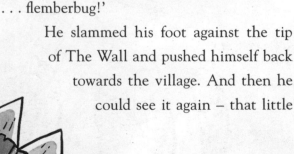

black dot, still skittishly circling
around in the sky as if it were lost.
Dev followed it around the western side
of the mountain, over the scrapyard, to
where the rock face sloughed away in a
vertical drop.

Just a little further. Dev gritted his teeth.

The flemberbug came to rest on a grass-tufted pillar, a thin slice of rock so tall and perilous it would be unreachable to anyone except a boy wearing chicken wings. Dev arrived seconds behind, his hands scrambling to grip the grass as he hauled himself up onto his knees. His arms felt like they were on fire. His lungs felt like they could burst.

And a surge of excitement crackled up his spine.

'CAUGHT you!' he wheezed with delight, slamming the jar down upon the flemberbug. It blinked back at him, inquisitively. Then its beautiful

blue wings quivered out and its chubby, transparent body padded back and forth, with one rather sad-looking leg trailing behind.

'Oh no! You're hurt!' Dev carefully, very carefully, tilted the jar and screwed on its lid. 'I promise I'll be careful with you, Limpy. How's that for a name? Limpy. Limpy the flemberbug!'

Suddenly, a sharp gust caught Dev's wings, yanking him backwards and slamming him into the mountainside. He gripped the jar handle between his teeth and, with all the strength he could muster, launched himself back into the air.

But his wings weren't working. At least, not as before. Something inside the frame had broken. He flapped as hard as he could, struggling to keep on top of the breeze. Leaning left as he tried to steer right.

'Would you get *away* from my scrapyard?!' A man waddled between the rolling mounds of twisted metal below. His clothes were smeared black with oil, his face squished beneath a helmet of welded metal. It made his already furious face look even furiouser.

'Schorry, Perschy!' Dev shouted down through clenched teeth. 'I schink I broke my wingsch!'

Percy gestured wildly towards the scrapyard furnace, inside of which a huge fire roared, belching thick black smoke from each of its four tall chimneys. Dev struggled to glide between them, but only avoided one column of smoke by turning into another, and suddenly it was all around him. Racing into his lungs, burning his throat with every spluttering cough. He spun around. And around. And around and around and then suddenly . . .

The clear blue sky.

The whole mountain swung into view below his feet.

Lower Eden, Middle Eden, Upper Eden. Treetops like tiny paint splots. Rivers like whisper-thin veins. A network of roads and alleys threading between hundreds and hundreds of tiny little rooftops.

'It'sch beautiful!' he gasped.

And then he started plummeting back down towards it.

2
A Little Faith

The rooftops of Middle Eden spun up towards Dev in a dizzying spiral. His face began to stretch, a thin line of spit trailing across his cheek, his body flapping around helplessly like a doll thrown into the waves of the sea.

Then he remembered something.

He slammed a fist onto the straps of his backpack and in an instant it all ballooned out around him.

'SCHANK YOU, PORTABLE AIRBAG!' he yelped, thudding into the rooftop of Gristle the Butcher's. He bounced back into the air, across a few

INVENTION 497: Portable Airbag

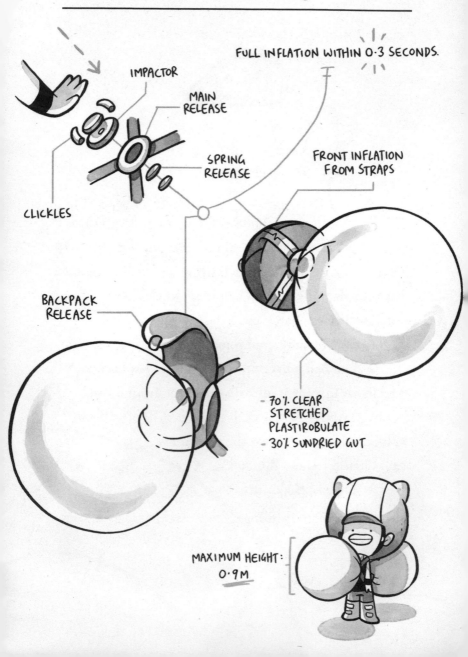

FULL INFLATION WITHIN 0·3 SECONDS.

IMPACTOR

MAIN RELEASE

SPRING RELEASE

FRONT INFLATION FROM STRAPS

CLICKLES

BACKPACK RELEASE

- 70% CLEAR STRETCHED PLASTIROBULATE
- 30% SUNDRIED GUT

MAXIMUM HEIGHT: 0·9M

more rooftops, before finally crashing down onto the cobbles of the marketplace.

'Dev's back from space!' Sam called out, as he and the other three Space Fleet cadets ran towards him. They helped Dev up and dusted him down.

'It's OK,' he wheezed, struggling to stuff the portable airbag back down. 'I'm OK. I'm alive!'

He patted himself down just to double check.

'DEV!' his mother's voice wheezed from across the street. She barged through the cluster of Space Fleet helmets, wrapping her arms around Dev's head. 'Don't ever, EVER, do anything as crazy as that again.'

'It worked though, Mum!' Dev grinned. 'I got a flemberbug!'

The jar spun on the ground by his feet. Limpy *bonk-bonk-bonked* around inside. Dev picked it up, fussing over his little friend, tapping the glass to check if he was all right.

Limpy turned away in a sulk.

'Flemberbugs always know when to come to our village.' Dev smiled. 'The exact same time every year! I'm going to find out *how* they know, and then I'm going to write a book about it.'

His mother took the jar with one hand, and pinched his lips shut with the other. 'You're going to do no such thing. You know full well that B-double-O-K-S aren't allowed in Eden. The Mayor would have it confiscated immediately.'

But Dev barely heard her. He had pulled away, and was hopping around, flapping his arms furiously, his face scrunched up in sheer delight. 'I FLEW!' he

yelped, as Space Fleet giggled and hopped around
with him. 'Just like a Flemberbug! High above the
rooftops. I flew! I FLEW!'

The giggling became laughter which, some-
how, became chicken noises, to which even Dev's

mother raised a smile. Then, one by one, Space Fleet tumbled to the floor, red faced, doubled-up in hysterics, until only Dev was still hopping.

Hop.

Hop.

And then – WHAM! He slammed his heels into the ground with just the right amount of pressure to activate his cheese boots.

A sickeningly loud SPLUTCH! echoed around the marketplace.

Dev turned slowly, reluctantly. Behind him, Zerigauld Sourface's Antique Shop was buried beneath a thick layer of three-month-old cheese. Dev stared in horror at the cheese-covered sign, dripping onto the cheese-covered antiques stacked in front of the cheese-covered window. And the cheese-covered door, blown open by the force, only to reveal all the shop's cheese-covered contents inside.

His stomach dropped like a lump of cheese thrown into a cheese river.

'I think I'm in trouble,' he sighed.

'Oh, Dev,' his mum said, pulling her scarf up over her nose.

Then, quick as a flash, Dev's frown spread into a wide, excited smile.

'I can fix it though . . .' he said. And before his mother could protest, he was squinting up at the sky, then down to his shadow.

'Half-seven. Hmm. Zerigauld doesn't open his shop until eight. That gives us half an hour to clean up his shop before he notices . . .'

On the outside, Dev looked thoughtful, tapping

a finger against his bottom lip. But inside his heart was blazing like a hundred suns, the thrill of a new challenge rippling through his body.

A new problem to solve.

A new *thing* to *fix*.

He clonked his fist against the side of his helmet. The top opened and a large glowing lightbulb poked out. It gave off a gentle heat, just enough to warm Dev's head, to stir a few more ideas around inside his brain.

He sank to the ground, cross-legged, resting his chin on his hands, staring at all the shops around  the marketplace. The old wooden carts. The humming power lines that criss-crossed between the trees. He looked over to the grassy bank in the middle of it all. The stone fountain, carved in the shape of a fish being sick, with water belching out of its mouth and splashing into the pool below.

Big, sparkling droplets of water.

All . . . that . . . *water.*

'THAT'S IT!' Dev jumped back to his feet, the bulb disappearing into his helmet. 'I know how I can fix this!'

His mother looked at him suspiciously. Dev grinned a wide, wide smile.

'I'm going to need a carrot.'

3
The Carrot is Important

'Dev's going to fix it!' Sam jumped up and down on the spot.

'Please, Dev.' Dev's mother's voice was sterner now. 'Not another dangerous invention.'

'Dangerous? Pfft! As if!' Dev wafted his hand as though the word itself was a bad smell. Then he crouched down in front of Sam and whispered in his ear. 'What I have planned IS going to be dangerous. Very, VERY dangerous. Do you think Space Fleet are up to such a *dangerous* mission?'

'Y-you want us to help?' Sam said as Space Fleet huddled around him.

'Yes I do!' Dev stood tall, and held his fist against

his chest. 'While I, Lieutenant Dev, am on MY mission, Space Fleet will have a mission of their own. Are you WITH ME?'

'We're WITH YOU!' they all cheered in unison.

'Excellent, now . . . hang on. Didn't there used to be more of you?'

Sam's smile fell off his face. 'There used to be loads.'

'Space Fleet had twenty-seven cadets last year,' Alice, the tallest member of Space Fleet, moaned, her cardboard-box helmet just balancing on top of her head. 'But none of our missions to go into space have worked, so . . .'

Reginald, a colander wedged onto his thick curly hair, huffed defiantly. 'So they aaaall left. Well, GOOD. We din' want them anyways.'

Arto, the smallest of them all, who had drawn all over her own face for some reason, frantically waved her arms. 'We Space Feet! SPACE FEET!'

'SPACE FEET!' They all joined in, stomping around in a circle before collapsing in a fit of giggles.

'Well, Space Feet, you're more than enough,' Dev beamed. 'These are your orders, and I expect you to follow them to the letter!'

He knelt beside Sam and whispered in his ear. Then he did the same to Alice, then Reginald, then Arto.

'Do you all understand your missions?'

'Yes, sir! Space Fleet, fall in line!' Sam cheered, hardly able to contain himself. 'We have our orders!

Meet back here in TWENTY MINUTES!'

'Go!' Dev grinned. 'For the sake of the galaxy! Go. GO!'

And with that, each cadet ran from the market-place. A trail of excited giggles echoing in their wake.

'Dev.' He felt his mother's hand on his shoulder. 'Promise me you won't—'

'I'll be back! With a carrot!' Dev shouted triumphantly, spinning on his heels and running down the narrow alley beside Zerigauld's shop.

'The carrot is important!'

The alley narrowed, and narrowed more, before suddenly opening up into Absolom Lane with all its delicious-smelling food shops. Dev leapt over barrels and crates, hop-scotched through a gaggle of honking geese, paused for a moment, to marvel at a tall stack of marshmallows in one of the windows, before swinging a hard left down into the cooler shadows of Pickety Road.

Down here, the streets were lined with stalls and tables, each selling something completely different from the last. Brooms and brushes at one. Miniature carved pigs at another. Every size and shape of duck whistle you could ever need at another.

The stall Dev was after looked old and tired. The vegetables stacked on it looked old and tired. Its owner, Ventillo, Dev's grandmother, well she was the oldest and tiredest of all. Small, huddled up in blankets behind the table, her cloudy eyes made huge by a pair of thick glasses. Her skin all cracked like dry mud. Wild purple hair spilling out from beneath her helmet.

'N-N-Nonna!' Dev stammered, trying to catch his breath.

'Dev?' Ventillo muttered. 'If this is about coming round for dinner, tell your mother I will. Sometime. End of the year maybe.'

'No, I need a carrot, Nonna.'

'Not a plum?' Ventillo's bony hand felt its way across the stall. Passing over the dark-blue plums.

Landing on the pears. 'Plums are good this week. Not too bruised. Are these plums?'

'A carrot.' Dev picked up the least withered carrot he could see.

'Peach.' Ventillo smiled, holding up a potato. 'They're good for you, Dev.'

'No, honestly, a carrot. I don't have much time. I just need this carrot.'

'I suppose it's better than nothing. Fine, a carrot.' She pulled her blankets tighter, all her bangles and bracelets clattering as she did. 'What'll you trade me for it?'

Dev rummaged around in his pockets. 'I have . . . a few cob screws, old wire, um . . .'

'No use to me.'

'Please! It's just a carrot.'

'Every carrot is important.' Ventillo snatched the carrot back, placing it amongst the apricots. 'You'll get no family favours here.'

'Fine. FINE! Here, how about this?' Dev grabbed the potato and pressed a cob screw into its skin. He then picked up a banana, stuck his other cob screw into it and connected them both with the wire thread.

Instantly, the banana began to glow.

Ventillo's eyes glistened, and her thin lips fell open. 'My boy, that's the most beautiful thing I've ever seen,' she gasped, reaching out and taking the banana from him.

'It's science!' Dev grinned, picking up his carrot. 'Energy from one, feeding into the other. And now you have a light-up banana!'

INVENTION 498: The Banana Light

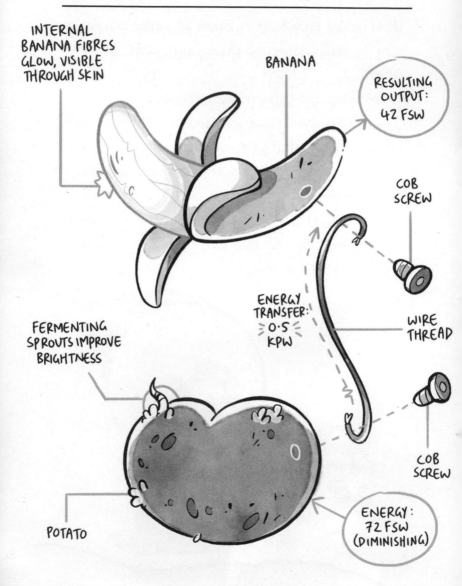

INTERNAL
BANANA FIBRES
GLOW, VISIBLE
THROUGH SKIN

BANANA

RESULTING
OUTPUT:
42 FSW

COB
SCREW

ENERGY
TRANSFER:
0.5
KPW

WIRE
THREAD

FERMENTING
SPROUTS IMPROVE
BRIGHTNESS

COB
SCREW

POTATO

ENERGY:
72 FSW
(DIMINISHING)

LIGHT PER LARGE POTATO: 36 MINUTES

Ventillo didn't reply. Didn't even look up. Didn't look anywhere except at her marvellous banana.

'Thank you for the carrot!' Dev cheered, continuing on down the road. Towards the lower parts of Eden.

Towards part two of his amazing plan.

The part he wasn't particularly looking forward to.

4
Bastor

Dissler's the Chemist. Boggarty's Clocks. Handel's Helmets and Helmet Accessories. This far into Lower Eden, the buildings were stacked so high they blocked out the sun, casting the valley into a deep gloom. Dev could feel goose bumps on his skin, but he wasn't sure if they were from the cold or his nerves.

Smoke rose from one of the buildings ahead. Dev peered around its large open doorway, a great warmth flushing into his cheeks.

'B-Bastor?' He called out. 'I . . . I need to borrow . . . something . . .'

Bastor the blacksmith was hunched over his workbench. His back looked like a bag full of conkers, all knotted muscles, which slid around and locked into place as he turned. Two huge, blackened arms folded across his chest. He was bald up top, but had a thick black beard hiding the lower half of his face. And what a face it was. Weathered and beaten, like a permanently annoyed tortoise.

Bastor the furious, knotted, permanently annoyed tortoise.

Dev ducked behind a rack of hand-crafted swords.

'Just the person I wanted to see.' Bastor smiled. 'I would value your opinion!'

He walked across the dirt floor, past the axes on the walls, the shields, the tools. Bowing underneath the low rafters he pulled on some thick gloves, picked up some pincers and lifted a small pot out from the fire.

Dev gulped. 'My . . . opinion? You don't want to shout at me instead?'

'Shout at you?' Bastor chuckled. 'Why on earth would I shout at you?'

'There's usually a reason,' Dev grumbled. '*Dev,*

don't turn that thing on in here. Dev, put that sword down . . .'

'Dev, put that sword down,' Bastor sighed.

Dev hadn't even noticed he had picked one up. It clanged loudly as he dropped it.

Bastor took a deep breath and continued, in as calm and as quiet a voice as he could manage. 'I've been working on this.' He walked the pot back over to the bench in the middle of the room and tilted it. A shimmering, silver liquid poured out, pooling into a heart-shaped stone cast.

'Do you think she'll like it?' Bastor cleared his throat. 'Amy, I mean?'

Dev scrunched his nose up. 'You made this for my mum?'

'Well, um . . . maybe. Yes.'

'What does it do?'

Bastor's face folded into a succession of expressions, each more thoughtful than the last. 'It, uh. It, well, it. It . . . It's just nice,' he finally shrugged.

'Oh, OK.' Dev smiled cheerfully. 'Well, that is true. It *is* nice.'

An awkward silence filled the air between them.

'FERVUS!' Dev suddenly remembered. 'That's what I came here for. Can I borrow Fervus? Just for a bit? Please?'

'Fervus?' Bastor's forehead creased up. 'Whatever for?'

Dev made his way behind the forge and crouched beside the tall red curtain in the corner. 'He's going to help me fix my mistakes.'

'Did Amy say this was OK?'

'Probably . . .' Dev took out the carrot and waggled it beneath the curtain. A small pink nose snuffled out. Its nostrils flaring as it *niff-niff-niffed* towards the carrot, before the rest of its white furry snout followed behind.

'Come out, Fervus.' Dev smiled, careful to hold the carrot just far enough away.

Hearing his name, Fervus the tiny goat tottered out into the light. He gave himself a big shake, ruffling out his fur, before finally opening his big black eyes and staring up at Dev.

'Well, OK, but please look after him.' Bastor nervously patted Fervus's horns. 'Some of us didn't have kids, y'know. Some of us had goats instead.'

Suddenly, Dev's mum screeched to a halt outside the open doorway. Dev instinctively ducked down behind the bench, bundling Fervus under his arm and peering out at his breathless mother.

Her hair was wild. Her cheeks were red. 'Bastor,'

she wheezed through a polite smile. 'Did . . . did Dev come in here?'

Bastor fiddled with the strings of his apron. 'Amy! Wh-what a lovely surprise . . . to see you. H-how are you today?'

'DEV. I thought I saw him come in here.'

'I-it's a *lovely* day,' Bastor stammered. 'I'm guessing. I mean, I spend all day here in the dark, so who knows, it could still be last week for all I know.'

He laughed a weird shrill laugh, before accidentally knocking a row of coal shovels off the wall. They hopped across the ground, clanging loudly together. Bastor apologised seven times.

Dev took his chance.

He scurried under the bench, skidding out behind his mother. He was running up the road before she had even noticed – back through the corridors of Lower Eden, up and into the sunlit Middle Eden streets.

Back into the marketplace.

His legs aching, he slumped down in front of

Zerigauld's cheese-covered antique shop. A crowd had begun to gather, covering their noses against the stinky cheese smell. Sam barged through them, proudly holding a large oily mechanical pump in the air.

'Commander Sam, reporting for duty! I got it, Dev! From one of the village generators, like you asked. Mission complete!'

'Excellent work, Commander!' Dev saluted and Fervus bleated from under his arm, at which Sam squealed with delight.

Then the crowd parted for Reginald. He was pushing Alice along in a wheelbarrow, her arms filled with a variety of long floppy tubes. 'Mission complete!' he puffed, heaving Alice up and onto the ground.

'Hoi!' she yelled.

'We went to your workshop to get these.' Reginald clanged his hand against the colander on his head. 'Wheelbarrow and tubes. I only stopped for two rests, and one toilet.'

'This is great; this is all great!' Dev put Fervus on the ground, lifted the pump and placed it in the wheelbarrow. He then strapped it down and plugged the thicker tubes into its side.

'Mishun compeet!' Arto's tiny voice yelled out, as she staggered between the crowd's legs. Her item was a large wooden wheel, larger than she was, hiding all but her feet.

'Ah, the last piece. A cartwheel. Brilliant work, Arto!' Dev smiled, taking the wheel. Arto's hair was full of leaves and twigs, her face scuffed. But she beamed proudly through all four of her teeth.

'And just in time, it's aboutttt . . .' Dev stared intently at his shadow on the ground. '. . . ten to eight. Not long till opening!' And with that he set to work, bending pipes, plugging things into other things, battering everything together, and hanging the carrot up in front of it all. Within minutes the whole contraption was finished.

Well, *nearly* finished.

He grabbed the thickest, longest tube of all and ran it from the back of the pump, up across the grass and into the fountain. He felt a fire begin to swell inside his heart. 'This could work,' he chuckled, hopping back towards his contraption. 'This could actually, actually work.'

Then he saw his brother, and every drop of enthusiasm suddenly drained away.

'I could have guessed it was you who caused all this cheese.' Santoro was dressed in his Youth Guild uniform – feather-garnished helmet, long blue tunic and smart, buckled boots. 'Your silly experiments usually only endanger yourself, but this time? You've damaged poor Zerigauld's shop. You're a public nuisance. And The Guild can't tolerate such things.'

'I'm *trying* to fix things,' Dev grumbled.

A scowl formed beneath Santoro's floppy purple fringe.

Other, older, Guild members huffed and puffed their way into the marketplace. They were the every-day shopkeepers, the traders, the clerks, now dressed in their blue tunics and waving thin swords, just like they had when Dev flew too close to The Wall.

Oh great, Dev sighed. *Now everyone's coming.*

He picked Fervus up and held him over the cart-wheel. The little goat's nose twitched towards the carrot.

Niff! Niff!

His legs started running in mid-air.

Niff! Niff! Niff niff niff!

'Dev!'

Both Santoro and Dev turned to see their mother staggering back up the hill. She managed to gasp a few words out.

'Dev . . . what . . . are . . . you . . . *up to?*'

'I'm trying . . .' he repeated, '. . . to *fix* things.' And without waiting for a reply, he dropped Fervus inside the thick rim of the cartwheel. Fervus, intent on getting to the carrot dangling just inches in front of his nose, surged forwards. His legs turned the wheel. The wheel powered the pump.

The machine rumbled into life.

5
The Goat-Powered Washtopus

'I'll call it . . . a Goat-Powered Washtopus!' Dev shouted over the clatters and the clangs and the *chugga-chugga-chuggas*. 'A whole new concept in cleaning! It will rid a building of cheese within minutes!'

Beneath her Guild helmet, Rosa Mildew looked worried. 'H-how does it do that?'

'Yeah, Dev,' Santoro scoffed. 'How, exactly?'

Dev didn't have a chance to reply. The long tube running from the machine to the fountain had already started writhing around between his feet. Great bulges of water squeaked along it, squeezing into the pump, firing its pistons at a furious

INVENTION 499: The Goat-Powered Washtopus

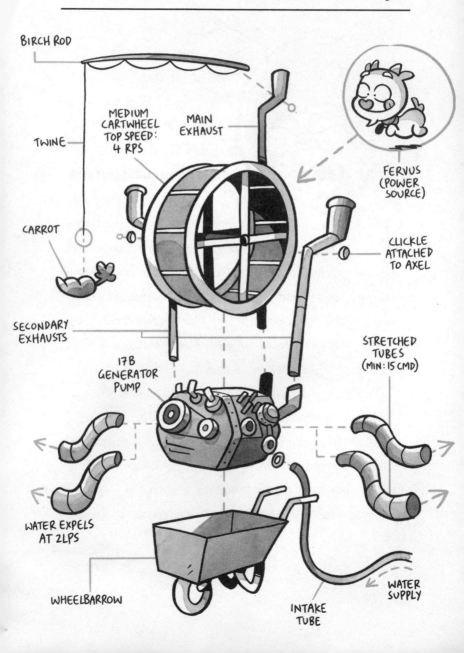

BIRCH ROD

MEDIUM CARTWHEEL TOP SPEED: 4 RPS

MAIN EXHAUST

TWINE

FERVUS (POWER SOURCE)

CARROT

CLICKLE ATTACHED TO AXEL

SECONDARY EXHAUSTS

17B GENERATOR PUMP

STRETCHED TUBES (MIN: 15 CMD)

WATER EXPELS AT 2LPS

WHEELBARROW

INTAKE TUBE

WATER SUPPLY

speed. Steam hissed out. The crowd shrieked and took a collective step back.

"'ERE! WHAT ARE YOU ALL DOING OUTSIDE MY SHOP?'

Zerigauld Sourface's bent, scrawny body appeared in the doorway.

Just then, the four arms of the Washtopus stiffened and cold water *SPLOOSHED* out at high speed. One blast propelled Zerigauld backwards with a yelp, another hissed along the front wall, knocking a variety of cheese-covered antiques spinning into the road.

'It's working!' Dev gasped. 'The Washtopus is cleaning Zerigauld's shop!'

Every inch of his skin prickled with pride, as he stood back to admire his amazing invention. It was noisy, sure, and a little heavy-handed, but oh *boy* was it doing the job.

'What's this big old thing then?'

Dev caught sight of his grandmother, *squelch-squelch-squelching* her way through the watery mist.

'I'm *cleaning*.' Dev beamed.

'Well aren't you being a good lad today? First my light,' she tapped the glowing banana taped to the front of her helmet. 'And now this. You deserve a reward.'

'Not at all, Nonna!' Dev laughed. 'I'm just glad to help!'

'Nonsense, one good turn deserves another. Here, since you like them so much, take as many as you want.'

She held out a crate with stack upon stack of bright orange carrots inside.

Dev's eyes widened in horror.

'No more carrots, they'll distract the goat!' He pushed the crate back towards her, hoping Fervus hadn't caught a whiff. 'I really don't need any more. Please, you keep them.'

'No no no, you were all excited about carrots. Take some,' Ventillo insisted.

'Perhaps it's not the best time, Nonna.' Santoro appeared, sliding one arm around Ventillo's shoulder, and with the other he took charge of her crate. 'The marketplace is a little . . . *busy* at the moment. Let me walk you, and your carrots, back home.'

Ventillo protested, but Santoro took charge, and he calmly led her away.

Dev exhaled with relief. A few moments later Commander Sam emerged from the crowd, staring in terrified fascination at the Washtopus.

'Is it . . . an *alien?*' he gasped.

'Sort of.' Dev smiled.

'He said yes!' Sam shouted back towards the crowd as Reginald barged his way through.

'ATTACK IT WITH CARROTS THEN!' he yelled,

clutching a carrot in each hand.

Why do you have . . . Dev didn't have time to finish the thought. A loud bleat rose up from behind him, and with an enormous blast of water, the Washtopus propelled itself towards Reginald. What was once just a cute goat in a wheelbarrow was now a hungry machine working overtime, thick smoke pouring out from the ribs of its engine.

'The carrots!' Dev's body flushed ice-cold with panic. 'It's coming for the carrots!'

Reginald instantly lost his nerve, flinging his carrots away, skidding onto his knees and burying his face in his hands. The Washtopus swerved past with less than an inch to spare, then clattered at speed towards Arto and the carrot *she* was holding. That is, until she threw her carrot to Alice.

Fortunately for them all, another large shape came charging through the mist. A huge, hulking, permanently annoyed tortoise shape. Bastor, now changed from his soot-covered apron into the striped tunic of the Guild Leader. He leapt towards

Alice, huddling his huge body around her as the Washtopus smashed into his back, crumpling into a shower of sparks and splinters.

Still this didn't stop the beast, now concealed inside a huge billowing cloud of smoke, crackling and sparkling like a thunderstorm as it reversed at speed towards Dev. He leapt out of the way and then ran alongside it, diving into the smoke, gripping onto the wheelbarrow, using all the strength he had left to haul himself up. He clawed over the hot, growling pump towards the wheel, reaching to pull Fervus out.

And as he did, he saw something up ahead.

Mina.

Her teddy bear tucked underneath her arm.

A carrot between her shaking hands.

6
The Great Hall

Twelve minutes later, Dev was being marched along the streets by a tight huddle of Guild members. Some held onto his arms, some his scarf, others carried broken bits of the Washtopus. Bastor led them all towards the Great Hall. They hauled Dev up each step, dragging him between its towering pillars, and through its large metal-studded doors.

The procession then came to a halt and pushed Dev to walk on alone.

Gingerly, he put one foot in front of the other. Bit his lip. Stared straight ahead. He walked towards the huge smouldering stone hearth at the darker end of the hall, stopping when he caught sight of the

bear's head mounted above it. Its mouth hanging open in a snarl. Its teeth, glistening in the low light.

He felt a chill across his arms. He looked to his right, at the line of shields across the wall, each bearing the sword and hammer emblem of the guild. And to his left, a line of tall windows, shuttered, sunlight creeping in around the edges.

A sharp cough. It was Santoro. He nodded Dev towards a large wooden chair in the middle of the room. Usually Dev would resist being told what to do by his brother, but not this time, not with this shivering unease in his belly, and so he dutifully trudged towards it. His feet squelched with every step. Loudly. Ominously. Echoing high up into the rafters. And then there were other footsteps shuffling in around him. Whispering. Helmets clonking together. Villagers, filling the shadows.

All keen to watch the show.

Dev sat. The whispering faded away. Not because it had stopped, but because his heartbeat was now the loudest noise in his ears.

'All stand,' a voice boomed. 'All stand for me. The Mayor. All stand for the Mayor.'

Mayor Bumblebuss always reminded Dev of a slug. A huge, lolloping slug. His big lumpy body swayed from side to side as he barged through the crowd, his robes dragging behind him like a gross trail of slime. His ridiculously oversized, fur-edged helmet was studded with gems, which shone like large rolling eyeballs.

Dev shuddered.

The Mayor wheezed towards his table. He slammed down a thick pile of papers and sank into the throne behind it. His shoulders heaved with each and every laboured breath.

'Shutters!' he puffed, and Guild members either side yanked on two long cords hanging from the ceiling. A succession of shutters fwip-fwipped up, as daylight blazed in through the windows and suddenly, unfortunately, the full horror of the Mayor was there for all to see.

His bloodshot eyes, buried under the weight of two enormous fluffy white eyebrows. His nose, wide and swollen, like it had been stung by a hundred bees. His mouth, drooping at either side, with spittle shining in each corner. There was something monstrous about the Mayor's face. Something that unnerved Dev to his core.

He gulped, clasping the arms of his chair.

The Mayor grabbed the large clock hanging from a chain around his neck, glanced at it, and sighed.

'Tick, tick, tick, time waits for no one.' The Mayor's bushy white moustache billowed out with each word. 'Let's get this done. Ten minutes, nine if you plead guilty.'

He peered over his bee-stung nose at the loose papers below him.

'Dev P. Everdew, of the noted Everdew family. One surviving parent. The other, well . . .'

He glanced up to the wall. There, beside the huge framed painting of himself, looking fine and splendid in his shiniest jewellery, was a smaller painting. This man wore a Mayor's robes too, but his were thinner, more discreet. He smiled back at Dev with a warm, knowing smile. A smile that calmed Dev's nerves, if only for a moment.

'Hi, Dad,' Dev whispered.

'Your father's not here, is he,' the Mayor sniffed, haughtily. 'And good, good that he isn't, he wouldn't want to see his son charged with destruction of property, goat stealing, reckless endangerment of life, irresponsible robot-building . . .'

'I built the Washtopus to *help*!' Dev mumbled.

The Mayor looked up from his papers. His eyes narrowed.

Dev sank a little further into his chair.

'From what I understand, you actually built it to cover up your previous mistakes?' A Guild member stepped forward holding a crate, from which the Mayor pulled out two cheese-soaked boots.

Dev wiggled his bare toes and took a deep breath.

'Those . . . those were my fault, sure. But the Washtopus was working fine, it was a great idea, until the goat . . . '

'Oh, are you blaming a GOAT?' The Mayor snorted.

A loud bleat echoed up from amongst the crowd.

'No! I mean, Fervus just wanted the carrots. Everyone seemed to have carrots . . .'

He paused. 'Hang on. Why *did* everyone have carrots?'

In his mind, he replayed what had happened. The Washtopus. Ventillo, with her crate of carrots. Santoro, shuffling her away. Only this time, in his memory, he saw Santoro glancing back at him. Only for a second. But it was there. It was definitely there. A smirk.

Through that silly floppy hair of his.

'Santoro did this,' Dev gasped, then frowned, then his whole face fell into a furious stare at the ground. '*Santoro* did this. He must have taken the carrots and handed them out to Space Fleet!'

'Oh, don't think I've forgotten about your brother.' The Mayor nodded over to Santoro, who stood, arms folded, against the wall. 'He should never have given you the chance to build this . . . "Washtopus". He should have brought you to this court as soon as you fell out of the sky.'

The Mayor tugged at the ruffles on his sleeve. 'No, your brother's biggest crime here is compassion.'

'WHAT?' Dev cried.

The Mayor squinted at Santoro. 'Why's he even in the Guild? He looks so young.'

Bastor cleared his throat. 'Youth Guild, sir. Top of his rank . . .'

'I don't much care, he's still a child,' the Mayor sniffed haughtily. 'And he dropped his guard. This is a first strike on your record, laddo. One more and you're out of the Guild.'

Santoro didn't flinch.

'Honestly,' the Mayor turned back around to face Dev, 'one brother causes all the trouble, the other just lets him get away with it. Disobedience must be in the blood. Percy, if you wouldn't mind.'

Percy from the scrapyard stepped out, his heavy metallic helmet still squashing his face in on itself. He was holding Mina in his arms. She buried her face in her teddy, her hair dripping a trail of water across the floor. Her left arm wrapped in bandages.

'Are you OK?' Dev asked. 'Mina, does it hurt?'

'Don't you say one word to her,' Percy snarled, as he walked behind the Mayor's table, perching Mina on the edge of it. She squeezed her red teddy bear, or at least, what was left of it, and stared glumly down at her boots.

'But I . . . I pulled Fervus out of the Washtopus! Just in time!' Dev cried.

'Just in time to bump my little girl into the fountain,' Percy spat. 'Landed badly, didn't she. My poor little girl. Soaking wet and crying her eyes out.'

'I'm so sorry.' Dev felt a tightness in his throat. 'Mina, I'm so, so sorry!'

The crowd began to chatter. The Mayor slammed his fists down on the table and let out a long, angry roar, wobbling all the rolls of fat under his chin.

'While Santoro's judgement in this may be questionable, ultimately it is you, Dev, who caused all the calamity, from beginning to end. And as such, it is you who must pay for it.'

'Throw him over The Wall. Into the Wildening.' Percy leant forwards. 'I'll carry him there myself.'

A chuckle rattled out from somewhere deep inside the Mayor. 'It's not a bad idea,' he mused. 'At least for a day. Two days. It might show you where this silly curiosity of yours will get you.'

'Over The Wall?' Panic rose inside Dev's chest.

The Mayor smiled, his cheeks pushing up so high that his eyes almost disappeared into the folds of his skin. 'We'll tie you by a rope, so you can't go too far,' he chuckled. 'Give you a little bell to ring if anything starts eating you.'

'You've heard the stories, haven't you, Dev?' Percy grinned. 'About why we built The Wall? And what lies out there . . . in the Wildening?'

Dev folded his arms in a desperate effort to stop himself shaking.

'*No one* goes beyond The Wall.' His mother's voice cut across the room. She marched out from the crowd, through the sunbeams, positioning herself between Dev and Percy. 'Least of all my *son!*'

'Maybe you shouldn't be encouraging all his ridiculous ideas then.' Percy gripped Mina even tighter. Then he lowered his voice to a growl. 'Wouldn't be surprised if he's finding them in books.'

'BOOKS?' The Mayor wobbled with rage again. 'We'll have no BOOKS in Eden.'

Amy unclipped Limpy's jar from her belt and showed it to the crowd. Limpy was fast asleep inside. 'No books, no laws broken. Dev's just curious about everything. This all happened because he was chasing a silly little bug.'

'A FLEMBERBUG?' Mayor Bumblebuss's voice

71

rattled through the bones of every person in the hall. 'You mean, they're here already?'

He rolled up his sleeve to reveal no less than three watches strapped along the length of his forearm. 'Big day coming up,' he blustered. 'Big, big day. You know that as well as anyone, Amy. And with only . . . forty-five hours and fifteen minutes to prepare for the most important day in our calendar, Middle Eden marketplace still stinks of CHEESE.'

'It's more like a fragrance,' Rosa Mildew offered.

The Mayor glared at her, and Rosa sank sheepishly back into the crowd.

'The flember won't *wait* for us to be ready.' The Mayor puffed up his chest, stepping out from behind his table. 'At the very moment when the flowers are in their fullest bloom, the grass is at its tallest, the Eden Tree is *humming* with life, do you think all that flember will give us a few extra minutes to hang our last bunting, or inflate our last balloon?'

Amy began to reply, but the Mayor shouted over her.

'NO!' he yelled. 'We must be READY! This whole village must be decorated in celebration, turned blue with flags and confetti. Which is why we can't allow for one excitable, STUPID little boy to smash through the middle of it, ruining the day for us all!'

'But I *love* Flember Day,' Dev protested. 'I don't want to rui—'

'Forty-five hours and thirteen minutes now!' The Mayor, cheeks flushed red, gripped his table and flung it over with a room-shaking crash. Papers whipped up into the air like autumn leaves. 'I will *not* have you doing *anything* to endanger my Flember Day.'

73

'Dev's only ever trying to *help*!'

'Well, he's not. He's ruining everything. As such, your boy is BANNED. BANNED from Flember Day!' Mayor Bumblebuss's whole body wobbled as he heaved himself out of his throne. 'If he must stay in our village, then he will be banned from ruining anything else we hold dear!'

Zerigauld leant out, clutching at the Mayor's robes.

''Ere, what about my shop?'

'And clean the old man's shop,' the Mayor huffed, pushing Zerigauld out of the way. 'PROPERLY, this time.'

'Banned from Flember Day?' Dev whispered.

'BANNED!' the Mayor called again from outside.

The word echoed around Dev's head.

Then it sank deep, deep down into the pit of his stomach.

7
Zerigauld Sourface's Antique Shop

Dev stood in a puddle of water and cheese. It soaked into his boots, in through the cracks where the canisters had once been attached. It chilled his toes, a festering, damp sensation, gross and squelching around his feet.

He barely noticed. He could only stare at the cheese-covered antique shop, his limbs sapped of energy, his mind replaying events over, and over, and over again.

'I just wanted to help,' he whispered.

'Yer daydreamin' again.' Zerigauld peered over his crooked wooden nose, his straggly eyebrow creasing in the middle, furrowing his little black eyes into a scowl. 'Always been yer problem, too much of a dreamer.'

He thrust a large vase at Dev, splattering lumps of cheese down his vest.

'Head full of ideas. None of 'em any good.' Zerigauld smirked as he wiped his cheesy hands on Dev's scarf.

Some of my ideas work, Dev thought.

Zerigauld leant in so close that Dev could see the thick waft of tobacco on his breath. 'Yous be careful, lad. This village 'as been very good to you, and you'd do well to remember it. Why's your cheeks bulgin' like that?'

Dev couldn't hold his breath any longer. He exhaled with a long, loud, 'HOOOOOOOO'.

Zerigauld jerked back, arching his eyebrow suspiciously.

'Yer a very weird boy, you know that. Very weird. But either way, you'll 'ave to come inside. Still plenty for you to scrub.'

'Inside?' A smile fluttered across Dev's lips as he stepped through the doorway. 'You've never let me inside bef . . .'

He fell silent, and the world outside was gone.

Dev had walked into a room full of treasures.

The walls were hidden behind an endless maze of sloping shelves. Stacked upon them were cases and trunks of all shapes and sizes, each bolted shut with heavily rusted padlocks. Below, were cabinets filled with glass bottles. Then cabinets filled with fabrics, all rolled up and crammed in together. On top of these, a selection of stuffed animals positioned as if in the middle of a fight – a lurching vole, a recoiling biddleshrew, a cheering mouse. And piled up in front, around and between it all, a variety of vases, pots, clocks, picture frames, candlesticks and battered musical instruments.

In fact, so distracted was Dev by the objects in front of him, he almost didn't see what was hanging above his head. A heart. A huge golden heart, bigger than he was. Suspended from the ceiling by chains.

Catching the sunlight and beaming it onto every fleck of dust that drifted past.

'NO YOU DON'T!' Zerigauld snapped. 'You keep yer eyes off of that 'eart. Not for yous, not for anyone. That ain't for sale.'

'Where did it come from?'

'Forget you seen it. I'll clean the cheese off it myself. You gots other things to be doin'.'

Zerigauld poked an old toothbrush into Dev's hand and spun him around to face the other wall.

'See all the teapots on these shelves?' He clonked his fist against Dev's head. 'Well delicately – *delicately* – you scrubs the cheese off of each one, y'hear me? And when I comes to check, I don't want to see no cheese *on* them, nor any cracks *in* them. Just one of these teapots is worth more than all the things you own in the world, y'understand?'

Dev quietly knelt down, picked up the first teapot and started to rub it with the toothbrush.

Out of the corner of his eye he could see Zerigauld dragging a ladder across the floorboards. His twig-like legs wobbled onto each step until he was crouching just below the heart. He pulled a rag from his pocket, spat on it and began scrubbing his most prized possession.

With Zerigauld well enough distracted, Dev put the teapot back in its place and started to shuffle along on his bum. From the teapots to the jewellery boxes to the broken toys, then on to the pyramid of specimen jars. He gleefully peered inside each one, scratching at their worn labels. He thought it might be exciting to try and identify the mould-covered creatures inside, but was a little disappointed when he did. They were the everyday caterpillars, moths and grass snakes of Eden village. Nothing he hadn't collected himself.

And yet, through the jars, he noticed something unusual. A long, dirty red curtain, barely concealing an archway in the wall.

Dev's curiosity spiked once more.

He checked again that Zerigauld was distracted and then set to work carefully pulling each jar away, reassembling them behind him, before shuffling under the curtain and inside the cold, dark archway. He clonked his helmet for a lightbulb, which plinked and fizzed, casting a little light against the narrow

walls.

Either side of him, running up and over his head, were strange, thin tiles. No, not tiles. These bulged. They had markings on them. They were rough to the touch.

They slid out when he pulled on them.

He could barely form the word with his lips.

These were b . . .

They're b . . .

'Books!' he finally squeaked.

Old books, new books, bits of books, huge books.

A cave of knowledge.

A FEAST for the brain.

He raised a trembling hand and ran his finger across their spines.

How to Make Nettle Jam . . . Techniques for Pig Wrestling . . . 591 Recipes for Cooking Rust-Beetles . . .

And then, two words that sent shivers across his skin.

8
Just Trying to Read a Book

The book was small, with a cracked blue cover. As Dev pulled it out, one of its rusting gold corners nicked against his thumb, drawing a thin line of blood. He didn't notice. He was too busy holding the book as if it were a priceless artefact. For there, on its cover, was a large golden F, and those two thrilling words again.

FLEMBER ISLAND.

A pained, horrified gasp rose up behind him, and Dev spun around to see Zerigauld Sourface, his bony fingers curling into even bonier fists.

'You 'orrible little snoop! You nosey little b-b-b-buttock!'

Instinctively, Dev hid the Flember Island book behind his back, before slowly stuffing it down into his trousers. 'I . . . I was just looking. I didn't think there were any books left in Eden . . .'

'There ain't! Mayor confiscated them all! Hates the things 'e does, says they encourage troublesome thoughts,' Zerigauld snarled. 'As if you needs any more of *those*!'

He clamped his fingers onto Dev's nose and dragged him through the shop. 'I couldn't get rid of them though,' he mused. 'I'm a collector y'see. I collect. It's in my blood. Can't well be destroying such artefacts.'

Dev saw a softness wash across Zerigauld's eyes, but then it was gone again.

'You'll not be telling anyone what you found 'ere,

you understand? Not *anyone*. Don't even be *thinkin'* about it.' He picked up a crate of cheese-covered candles. 'Ere, take these instead, and find somewhere to dump 'em. Somewhere discreet. And then come right back – there's still plenty to do.'

Dev lifted the crate to his chest. The thick, ripe stench of cheese once again filled his nostrils. He gagged as he carried it away from the marketplace, he dry heaved all the way down the hill, and his stomach *boilked* as he turned onto Bumnickle Lane. Finally, he could take it no more, and he guiltily rolled the crate into some hedges.

Then he looked around to make sure no one was nearby, hauled the book out from his trousers, and found a nice stone step to sit on.

'Maybe you'll show me what's over The Wall,' he whispered, chewing his bottom lip as he turned to the inside cover.

'Is that a book?' Beneath the awnings of his waffle shop, Arnold the waffle maker poked his big cheerful face through an open window. A cloud of delicious waffle smells billowed out around him, like a wonderful, sweet-smelling fart.

Dev slammed the book shut again, and shuffled himself on top of it. 'I just . . . I was throwing things away for Zerigauld. Stopped for a rest.'

Arnold tried to peer round Dev. 'He's got books in that shop, does he? Been years since I've seen one of them.'

Dev hurriedly tried to change the subject. 'Something smells good.' He smiled.

'Ah!' Arnold smiled, raising a dumpy finger in the air. 'That'll be the waffles!'

He disappeared back inside his shop. Within an instant he had reappeared in the doorway. In his bare hands he held a tower of waffles, whipped cream and small red berries all illuminated by a single sparkler. Syrup dripped through his fingers.

'On the house, for my most regular customer!'

His moustache pushed right up into his cheeks, and his bushy eyebrows waggled up and down. 'I call it the Flember Day Special,' he said, passing the waffles to Dev. 'I've been hiding away for weeks, not talking to anyone, absolutely *dedicated* to perfecting the recipe.'

Dev pinched off a chunk of the soft dough and bit into it.

88

'It's sprinkled with bobbleberries,' Arnold continued. 'You know, bobbleberries only grow at this time of the year.'

'Fur a monpfh,' Dev took another mouthful, 'then they burshht, but de sheedsh catcshh the wind and . . .'

A lump of waffle wedged in Dev's throat. Spots of colour flashed in front of his eyes. He lurched forwards, clawing at his neck, just as Arnold's palm slammed between his shoulders, propelling the lump up and out of his windpipe. It skidded along the cobbles like a stale bun across a pond.

'Goodness me!' Arnold flustered. 'You turned bright red for a minute there.

Almost thought you were a bobbleberry.'

Dev took a few deep breaths. Then he grabbed another lump of waffle and stuffed it into his mouth. 'Itsh just rilly delicioushh.' He grinned. 'Yer ver good at wahffles – *CHOMP!* – Arnold.'

Arnold looked at Dev, and shook his head.

'Well, there's still a bit more time to perfect the recipe before Flember Day.'

Dev's face fell, and his chewing slowed to a halt. *Flember Day.* Those words were usually a great source of excitement to him, but now they just hung like a dead weight around his neck.

'I'm not allowed at Flember Day,' he mumbled through a mouthful of half-chewed waffle. Then he swallowed, loudly.

'Ah, yes, I heard what happened.' Arnold apologetically twiddled with his apron straps. 'Sorry, Dev. That can't be a nice feeling at all.'

Dev tore off a bit more waffle, and pressed it into his mouth.

'Best you put that book back then, before anyone

else sees you reading it.' Arnold winked. 'You wouldn't want to make things worse for yourself.'

The BOOK. Dev shuffled back on top of it, as if that might make Arnold forget all about it.

Arnold patted him on the head, smiled sympathetically, and stepped back inside his shop. 'Shout if you start choking again,' he called out.

'Will do!' Dev saluted, another bobbleberry-covered chunk heading towards his mouth. He listened for the hiss and clunk of Arnold's waffle irons starting up again. Then he reached for the book. A few moments ago it had felt like a treasure, but now it just felt like a burden.

Something else to be told off for.

'I'll just have a quick look,' he sighed. 'Then I'll put it straight back.' But before he had a chance to even open it, the book slipped through his syrup covered hands. It dropped onto the ground with a thud, its covers fell open, and a bundle of torn, scrappy pages spilled out from inside.

If flember is a resource to be shared amongst all living things, CONNECTING us all, then the FLEMBERSTREAM is the pool from which we draw.

ALL IS BORROWED AND THEN RETURNED.

Larva

Pupa

Worm

Scuttlebug

F

...our experiments pro[...]
[...]THYST CRYSTALS
[...]ke coal, but catch[...]
[...]olours of the l[...]
quite b[...]

[...] quite
[...]ember
[...]er)
[...]yst

Flember[...]
LUNGS, br[...]
[...]a, and e[...]

[S]OURCE

[...]able as death
[...]us, it is an
[...]art of the
[...]process.

[...]
D[...]
F[...]
M[...]
hol[...]
fle[...]
thr[...]

[N] BODY

[...] flember, perhaps we
[...]ith ourselves. Our
[...] from a series of
SYSTEMS (lymphatic,
[...]mune, etc). Each is
[...]edicated, but works
[...] greater whole (us).

WHERE do we add flember to this list? Does it flow through us like blood, pumped by a mechanism similar to the **HEART?**

And HOW is it kept at a sustainable level - FOOD?

[...]emonstration
[...]action

[...]espans
[...]sting only
HOURS.

[...]orn, they reproduce,
[...]Flember is drawn,
[...]and returned to
[...]BERSTREAM.

continual + endless

[...]ANCE

[...]er cannot be
[...]ustable, it is
[...]rce and as
[...]ust have
[...]t (however
[...]able those

[...]erm
[...]us ↑
[...]rom
[...]ed.

Flember returns to the ground. The Flember[...]

The more pages Dev turned, the more they reminded him of his own sketches. A flurry of writing and drawings. Thoughts, frantic thoughts, the kind of thoughts that appear in your brain far faster than your hand can write them down.

These loose pages weren't about the island.

They were about an *idea*.

'What's *that*?' Mina's shadow appeared over the pages.

'Mina! Um, it's . . . it's nothing.' Dev grabbed the Flember Island book and slipped the pages back inside. Then he he leapt up and hugged her as carefully as he could.

'Are you OK? Your arm? Does it hurt?'

'Only a little bit. It smells funny too.' Mina raised her bandage-wrapped wrist under Dev's nose. 'Wiv the . . . lello . . . bean clothes.'

'Yellowbean cloves?' Dev laughed. 'Well, those'll help you get better. But we really shouldn't be talking, your dad would be angry.'

'You gotta fix my Boja Bear.' She held her red teddy

bear out towards Dev. It was a lumpen, sorrowful-looking thing. Its fur was damp and matted, laden with grit, and stuffing spilled out from the hole where its arm had once been. Where it had lost an eye, a turnip had been wedged into its eye socket.

'I'm really sorry I ran him over with the Wash-topus,' Dev sighed.

'You can fix him!' she beamed 'You *made* him. When I had bad dreams!'

'Boja Bear will scare the scares,' Dev chuckled, remembering Mina's delighted face when she first saw him. 'But you're older now, you can scare the scares away yourself.'

'But . . . Boja Bear.' She pressed Boja Bear into Dev's face, until its red fur was tickling up inside his nose.

'Mina – mmf – no.' He gently pushed her back. 'I can't do anything. I can't help you any more. Your dad would be furious if he even saw us talking.'

Mina's eyes began to glisten. Her bottom lip wobbled. 'But . . .' she protested. 'But I want to imbent things, just like you do. You fix things.' She waved Boja Bear in front of him. 'You can fix *him*.'

Dev turned away, and stared sorrowfully at the ground. 'I think you should fix him yourself,' he barely whispered, a lump forming in his throat. 'I'm sorry, Mina.'

She stood there for some time, waiting for Dev to turn back around. But he couldn't. He didn't have the strength to see her looking disappointed in him. Finally, she made a loud snorting noise, spun around and stomped noisily down the street.

'I'm best left alone,' Dev grumbled, allowing the book to open in his hands, and idly flicking through the pages. 'I'm busy anyway. I have things to do. First things first, I need to take this book back beforrrrre . . .'

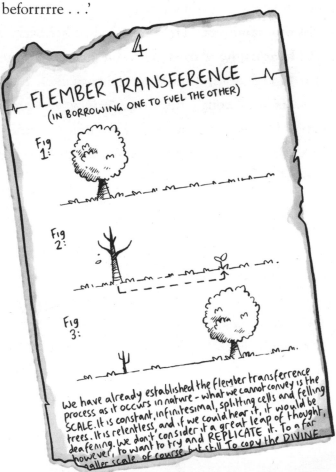

4

FLEMBER TRANSFERENCE
(IN BORROWING ONE TO FUEL THE OTHER)

Fig 1:

Fig 2:

Fig 3:

We have already established the flember transferrence process as it occurs in nature - what we cannot convey is the SCALE. It is constant, infinitesimal, splitting cells and felling trees. It is relentless, and if we could hear it, it would be deafening. We don't consider it a great leap of thought, however, to want to try and REPLICATE it. To a far smaller scale, of course, but still. To copy the DIVINE

Borrowing one.

To fuel the other.

The words leapt from the page, spiralling up into Dev's brain, firing every neuron they passed as if they were setting off a line of cannons.

His heart pounded.

All his hairs stood on end.

He turned, staring at Mina, at poor Boja Bear being dragged along the street, and a thousand different thoughts smashed together inside his head.

'I wonder . . .' He gripped the book tightly to his chest. 'I JUST WONDER!'

9
An Experiment

'See what it's showing?' Dev panted, holding the page up in front of Mina's nose. She sniffed a loud, snotty sniff, and shook her head.

Dev continued. 'But look at the *drawing*.'

Still nothing.

'Flember! It keeps the tree alive, but when the tree dies that flember passes onto something new!' He flicked through the pages. 'This book . . . It seems to be saying we could copy that process. Borrow flember from one thing, and put it into . . . '

He looked down at the red teddy bear in Mina's arms. 'Boja Bear is pretty tatty, you know. His stitching is coming apart, he's too flimsy to stand on his own.'

'You can fix him!' Mina smiled a huge, gap-toothed smile.

'I could fix him, yeah. Orrr . . . I could *improve* him.'

'Can he have three eyes?' Mina chirped, hugging Boja Bear tightly. 'And twelve arms?'

'I was thinking even *better* than that, Mina.'

'FIFTEEN arms?'

'Let's leave the arms.' Dev reached out for Boja Bear's paw. 'What if, instead, we could bring Boja Bear to *life*?'

Mina gasped. A long, longggg gasp, which at first made Dev's heart sing, but then seemed to be going on a little too long, so long he was worried she might pass out.

'This book, Mina! The book will tell me how to do it. How to turn Boja from this floppy, tatty teddy bear into a living, breathing creature!'

Finally, Mina breathed out with a loud *BHWOOOOOO!*

'A real-life Boja Bear to keep you safe.' Dev flinched, remembering her terrified face just before the Washtopus knocked her into the fountain. How she had dropped the carrot, and instinctively held Boja Bear out in front of her. Something, anything, to lessen the blow.

'You need someone to protect you,' Dev sighed. 'And I don't think that someone is me.'

'Boja Bearrrr!' she giggled. 'Will he dance? I wanna dance with him!'

'I think he might.' Dev patted the book. 'Dance, play, laugh and blow great big raspberries.'

'Not as loud as m—*thppbthhhhhhh*!' Mina started blowing one midway through her own sentence. Dev joined in with a laugh, and the air between them became a happy mist of noise and spit.

He took Mina's hand. 'To the – *thbbththhh* – workshop!'

Together, they *FRRPED*, *THPPPTBTHHED*, laughed, *PRPPPED*, giggled and *HONKKKKED* all the way down the narrow alleys of Lower

Eden, quietening down only as they passed Percy's Scrapyard and then resuming the raspberry blowing orchestra up, up along the cliff face. Before long they were back on lush grass, walking through the shade of the spindletrees. Then up the front steps of Dev's house, and giggling all the way inside.

The door to Dev's workshop opened with a long, loud creak. He took a  deep breath – familiar smells of rosemint, camphor and the smoky fumes of a few burnt-out experiments. Dev never felt like he was home until he could smell these things. Until he could see rack upon rack of bottles and jars lining the walls, all different shapes and sizes, all caked in dust. The labels long since worn away. Their contents long since forgotten. Crates, too, each filled to the brim with scraps of paper. The many thousands of

plans Dev had started, all the inventions he'd never have time to build. And scattered across the floor, so many *bits*. Bits of bicycle, bits of engine, bits of clock. Bits of bits. They looked, to the casual observer, to be thrown randomly around the workshop, but Dev knew where every bit lay. And where every bit could one day go.

Mina ran past, out onto the workshop balcony. 'Did you use this ramp to fly?'

'Sure did!' Dev smiled. 'I didn't have enough thrust though. The Cheese Boots weren't ready when I needed them! Not *stinky* enough!'

'Daddy drinks hibbicus beer and that smells horrrrible.' She pinched her nose, sticking out her tongue. 'You could use that!'

'Hmmm, hibbicus.' Dev thought about it as he walked over to his workbench. 'That *could* work.'

He cleared a space, opened the flember book and flipped through the loose pages straight to chapter four. 'But right now, we have other priorities!'

He tugged on the chinstraps of his helmet. As he

did, the pointed ears slid apart and a tangle of thin
metal arms folded out from inside, holding a variety
of magnifying glasses and spotlights which slotted,
one by one, in front of Dev's face.

'Tinkering Helmet, activated.' His magnified eyes
blinked down at a ridiculously excited Mina. 'Let's
get started!'

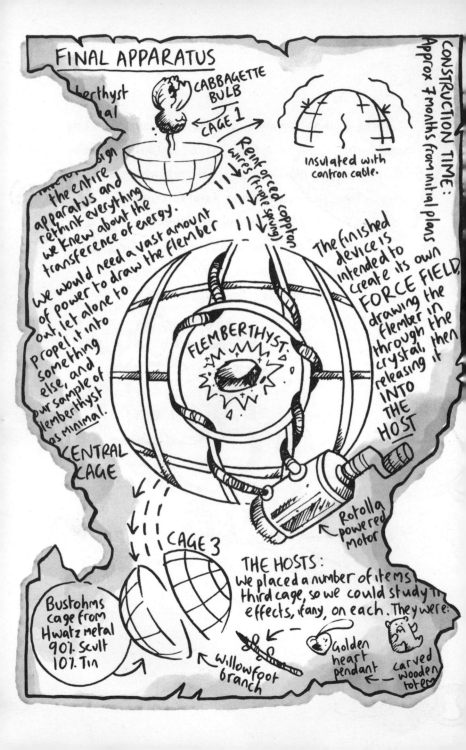

'Fascinating.' Dev grinned. 'I mean, I don't actually HAVE any of these things, but I'm nothing if not resourceful!'

He rooted through the cupboards below his workbench, throwing all manner of coils and springs across the floor before finally grabbing a bundle of wires, a silver plate, a birdcage, two clamps and an egg whisk.

'Mina, this book is amazing. First I thought it was about Flember Island, then about flember itself, but it's actually about BOTH of those things. The flember *in* the island!'

He hugged her up off the floor.

'Life, Mina! We can borrow some from the ground!'

Mina squealed with delight and

then, on Dev's instruction, picked a tiny whitedrop flower from the row of plant pots on the windowsill. Dev put her back down and placed the flower onto the silver plate, before carefully clamping one of the wires to its thin stem.

'I mean, it's not like we're doing anything different from what happens in nature,' Dev continued. 'This flower has already borrowed flember from the ground and it's . . . well, it's *storing* it. Then one day it'll give that flember back so new things can grow. It's all a big loop. Round and round.'

Mina nodded with the look of someone who didn't understand, but was still excited about absolutely everything that was happening. She picked up a screwdriver and waggled it in the air. 'I wanna help imbenting!'

'*Inventing*,' Dev replied. 'And we nearly have all we need . . .'

Dev studied the picture for some time. Then he pounced onto his shelves, climbed up to the very top and pulled out a small wooden chest. Inside, he kept stones – round ones, square ones, hard ones, soft ones, green and blue and every colour of the rainbow, every curious and unusual stone he'd ever found on his travels around the village.

He pulled out a misshapen lump of dark crystal, and held it up to the sunlight. Tiny flecks of colour danced around inside. 'This must be a flemberthyst.' He grinned, jumping back down. 'I just thought it looked pretty.'

'BOJA BEARRRR!' Mina suddenly yelled, raising Boja Bear above her, and stomping around in a circle. 'REAL . . . LIFE . . . BOJA . . . BEARRR!'

'Just a few more minutes,' Dev said, turning to the next chapter in the book. 'There are still a few more pages to read . . .'

GOLD

5

While our device HAD produced the desired results, namely extracting flember from one organism and passing it into another, there was one further unexpected discovery. One reaction we could not have anticipated!

INEVITABLE QUESTIONS ARISE

We chose the three test items for their predicted responsiveness to the process. In order of reaction, they are:

) foot branch ic, highly osive.

wooden

rganic ze, now . Unlikely o respond.

) Golden heart pendant - Inert, no response. How wrong!

Of all the items in the third cage, it was the most inanimate that had the most lasting reaction - the golden heart pendant. We expected gold to act like any other metal and be unaffected by the flember but instead, once the experiment was over, the gold STILL HELD the small amount of flember which had passed through it.

Could we then put flember-charged gold inside something else to power a larger body? We have a battery.

Light sparks of blue and white danced across it, around it, like +++ +++ miniature lightning storms. Flember radiation!

And yet, the flember itself appeared to be unable, or unwilling, to leave the gold. And it has remained there EVER SINCE.

CONCLUSION

We struck lucky in this discovery, and stumbled upon an entirely natural flember BATTERY.
Gold HOLDS THE FLEMBER, AS A CHARGE. It cannot use it, it has not the means, but it can, nonetheless, store

'Gold. Gold? Where am I supposed to get *gold* from?' Dev muttered.

'DEV, I'M SO EXCITED I MIGHT WEE.' Mina tucked Boja under one arm and tugged on her blue bunches, dragging them down in her fists.

'ME TOO!' Dev cried, slamming the book shut. 'We'll leave the gold out for now. So are you READY?'

Mina pulled her helmet goggles down over her eyes. 'LET'S GOOOO!'

They high-fived, then Dev turned to place the crystal inside the birdcage, before snapping the handle from the egg whisk and wedging it into the top. He then picked up the wire and threaded it from the clamp on the whitedrop flower into the birdcage, wrapping it around the bars and then out the other side.

'From one, to the other.' He nodded. 'Mina, if I may?'

Mina handed Boja Bear over to Dev. Dev removed the turnip from his eye socket and clamped the wire inside. Then he seated the bear beside the device.

The weird, cobbled-together device.

'Well then,' Dev chuckled as he pulled the straps of his helmet once more, and all the glasses, lights and twisted metal arms sprang back inside.

'Let's bring a teddy bear to life.'

INVENTION 500: Makeshift Flember Transference Device
(name to be decided upon)

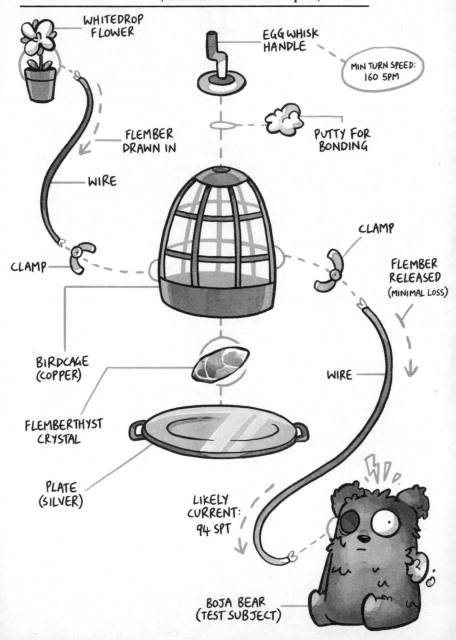

WHITEDROP FLOWER

EGG WHISK HANDLE

MIN TURN SPEED: 160 5PM

FLEMBER DRAWN IN

PUTTY FOR BONDING

WIRE

CLAMP

CLAMP

FLEMBER RELEASED (MINIMAL LOSS)

BIRDCAGE (COPPER)

WIRE

FLEMBERTHYST CRYSTAL

PLATE (SILVER)

LIKELY CURRENT: 94 SPT

BOJA BEAR (TEST SUBJECT)

10
An Awful Screaming

Dev turned the handle of his Makeshift Flember Transference Device (official name yet to be decided upon). The birdcage hummed. The flember-thyst crystal started to wobble.

'Faster!' Mina yelled.

He spun faster. The birdcage hummed louder. Faster. *Faster*. The wire to the whitedrop flower writhed and twisted. Faster. *Louder*. The silver plate rattled. The whole workshop began to rumble. All the jars and bottles clinked and clunked together. Louder. And faster. And *louder*. Dev gritted his teeth, his whole body buzzing like it was about to pop, his feet struggling to stay on the floor.

And then he saw it.

A soft, blue glow from the whitedrop's petals. Brighter and brighter, fizzing and glimmering, wafting out like a mist made of stars.

'FLEMBER!' Dev gasped.

The mist swirled down, around the clamp, then quickened along the wire. Through the bars of the birdcage and into the flemberthyst, lighting it up in a beautiful white glow. Then CRACK, the flemberthyst split; flember then crackled out and along the other wire, straight into Boja Bear's eye socket and disappeared down inside his body.

Dev's mouth fell open.

'YEEEEEEEP!' Boja Bear suddenly squealed. His face stretched out into a long, stunned horror. His one good eye rolled around in its socket. His legs thumped against the workbench.

'YEEEEEEEP!'

'Why is he screaming?' Mina turned pale. 'Dev, why is he screaming?'

'I . . . I don't know,' Dev gasped.

Boja Bear's eye stared back at them, his arm pawing at the space where his other arm should have been. Then suddenly he smiled, a sweet, calm smile, and he slumped backwards.

All the bright blue flember sparkled out through his fur, soaking down into the surface of the work-bench. Mina pulled her lifeless bear away and sobbed loudly into his fur.

'The flember!' Dev took a large empty bottle from

the shelf, as if he was trying to trap a spider. 'Where did it go? Where did it *go*?' He patted his hands around, before finally catching sight of it. Sparkling. Glowing. Dancing around the large golden F on the front of the flember book.

'We did it,' Dev's voice quivered. 'Mina, we caught some flember!'

He raised the book to show her. Mina stared back, her eyes glistening with terror, her toy bear hanging limply in her arms. She could barely choke out any words.

'He was screaming,' she whispered.

'I . . . we . . .' Dev opened the book, flicking through the pages as if searching for an explanation, but he couldn't look away from Mina. 'Maybe it was his arm. He was missing an arm, and an eye, maybe it hurt.'

The words felt weird to say.

Maybe it hurt.

Maybe an inanimate teddy bear *hurt*.

'H . . . he came to life,' Dev stuttered. 'He actually came to life.'

Mina started shaking as if she was struggling to hold back an absolute explosion of tears.

Dev brought a hand over his mouth.

'I've done it again,' he gasped. 'I've hurt you, *again*.'

Just then, the workshop door flew open and there stood Percy, heaving with rage. Without a moment's hesitation, Dev buried the flember book beneath a small pile of engine parts.

'WHAT'S GOING ON UP HERE?' Percy roared.

Mina lifted her goggles and ran over, burying her face into his oily apron, still wailing as he reached his huge arms around her.

Santoro slid past them both, smiling his thin, cruel smile at Dev.

'Your brother goes back in front of the Mayor,' Percy scowled.

'*I'll* take care of this,' Santoro replied.

'You're just a kid. A kid in a uniform.'

Santoro's hand reached back for the hilt of his sword.

'I am *Guild*,' he snarled.

Percy held Santoro's stare for as long as he could, before swinging Mina away and out of the workshop. 'Rotten apples,' he called out through the house. 'All of you. Rotten apples falling from a dead tree.'

Santoro waited until he heard the front door slam, before grabbing Dev's arm and jerking it up behind his back.

'I said, I'll take care of this.'

11
Santoro

Santoro's boots clipped Dev's heels all the way back to Zerigauld's antique shop. Dev, however, barely looked up from the path.

He could only think of Mina.

Zerigauld waited for them outside. He squawked about 'work ethic' and 'responsibility', while handing Dev a bucket of soapy water and a sponge. Dev knelt down, picked one of the many cheese-covered vases piled up in the doorway, and started scrubbing it.

Zerigauld watched over him for a moment, before clapping his hands together and smiling up at Santoro.

'Oh, since you's 'ere, Santoro, can I's interest you

in a new rapier sword? I know them silly Youth Guild swords is too flimsy for a *considerable* fighter such as yourself . . .'

Zerigauld hobbled back inside his shop, clattering through his crates and boxes.

Santoro ignored him, instead pressing the tip of his boot into a small lump of cheese on the floor, and smearing it into a crescent. 'You missed a spot,' he snarled.

It was enough to snap Dev out of his thoughts. He felt his cheeks flush red.

'I know it was *you* who gave Space Fleet those carrots, back in the marketplace,' Dev hissed. 'And you did it because you *knew* Fervus would go for them. The Washtopus was working just fine until you sabotaged it.'

He didn't wait for Santoro to respond. 'You just wanted to see me fail,' Dev muttered, scrubbing at the cheese. 'You only ever want to see me fail.'

'What's all this?' Zerigauld stepped over Dev, holding a long wooden casket. 'Stop blamin' your silly little inventions on other people, Dev. Ain't dignified. Look at your brother, 'ere, in all 'is finery. 'Is polished tan boots, the glor-r-r-rious blue and white stripes of Eden 'cross his tunic. Look how smart 'e looks. How respectable! And then look at yous.' His wooden nose pointed down at Dev. 'Baggy trousers. Scuffed knees! And yer 'elmet, wi' all bits fallin' out of it? I mean, honestly, who's goin' to take you seriously dressed like that?'

Dev's mouth went to protest, but his brain thought better of it.

Zerigauld opened the casket. ''Ere, Santoro, try this sword. It 'as an ivory hilt.'

Santoro twisted around to show Zerigauld the non-regulation sword strapped across his back. Its wide, rectangular blade made it look more like one of Gristle the butcher's over-sized meat cleavers. 'I have my own,' he growled.

'Course. COURSE.' Zerigauld smiled. 'For now. But you'll be Guild Leader soon enough, won't yous? Bastor might be all muscle, but he's no youngster, wi' all that soot in his lungs, puffin' an' a-wheezin'. 'E won't be in charge much longer. Fresh blood, tha's what this village needs, an' who better than you? You, wi' a gleaming new sword from old Zerigauld. At a discount rate, course.'

Santoro didn't even look at him. 'I'm here to guard Dev, nothing else.'

Zerigauld bowed and shuffled backwards, as if in the presence of royalty.

It was another few hours before Dev was finished. A few more hours for his mind to stew on everything that had happened today. The Wash-topus, Santoro and the carrots, the Mayor. The ban from Flember Day. The book too, and the bright, beautiful flember. Boja Bear's terrified screaming.

Poor, distraught Mina.

All these memories rolled round and round in his

head, taking it in turns to remind him how, for all his efforts to help, he only ended up making everything worse.

Here in the antique shop, however, he had finally managed to do some good. Every vase now glistened, every pot shone, every weird stuffed ferret thing was still a weird stuffed ferret thing, only now with all the cheese brushed out of its fur. Zerigauld carefully positioned each item back inside his shop until everything looked normal again. Better than normal, in fact. His shop was now cleaner than it had ever been before, complete with a fresh lemony scent in the air.

'Right, all done!' Dev pushed on his aching arms and stood up. His spine clicked loudly as he stretched, leaning all the way back, until he was staring at the shop ceiling.

At the golden heart glinting above Zerigauld's head.

'Took yous long enough,' Zerigauld snorted. 'Maybe this'll teach y'some patience, eh boy?'

'Y-yes . . .' Dev nodded, still staring at the heart.

The huge, shining lump of gold dangling just out of reach.

Gold.

Gold!

The one thing he'd left out of his flember experiment.

'What you waitin' for, some kind of thank you? Y'can shove it up your bum. It's gettin' late and you've already wasted too much of me precious time. Ger-rout!' Zerigauld scuttled towards him like a grumpy spucklepig, shooing Dev through the door and out into the street.

'Fiiiiiinally.' Santoro was stood outside, arms crossed. 'What took you so long?'

Dev stammered out a few indignant noises.

'Great, yeah, whatever.' Santoro yawned. 'Let's get you home.'

The warm afternoon sun had already begun to fade, burying itself behind the ocean and throwing delicate orange washes across the clouds. Lanterns *plink-plink-plinked* alight as Dev and Santoro walked beneath them, past the cosy glowing windows, through the delicious smells wafting out from each open doorway.

Then there was a loud noise and all the lights went out.

'GENERATOR!' someone shouted from the shadows.

'GENERATOR!' others began to call.

Santoro sighed, grabbing Dev's wrist, and yanking him across the marketplace. 'Come on,' he said. 'Guild duty.'

Dev broke free of his brother's grip but continued alongside him, down a side street, between grumbling residents and giggling children, until the path opened out onto a rocky peak. He peered over the edge at all the lights of Lower Eden twinkling below them.

'They're all fine down there, it must just be us.'

Santoro was staring at a large generator half-embedded in the rock face. Thick grey smoke spilled out from its *clunk-clunking* pistons. Something inside it fizzed and popped.

Dev stood beside his brother. 'I've fixed more of these than I can remember.' He smiled.

'So have I.' Santoro swung his boot forward into the generator's metal roll cage. Sparks burst out over them both. He kicked again. And again. Gritting his teeth as he lashed out. Denting it. Breaking it.

'Wait, wait, wait!' Dev pulled him back. 'A generator is an engine. Energy goes in, energy comes out, it's all a very delicate process. You can't just *attack* it!'

'I can.' Santoro kicked it again. 'I am.'

'Santoro, stop it!'

'*You're* not going near it, if that's what you're thinking.'

'Let me try. I can hardly break it any more than you!'

Santoro stared at Dev for a moment, then stepped back.

'Go on then. Use that supposedly *amazing* brain of yours.'

Dev knelt down in front of the generator and

traced his fingers around its casing.

'Orofractor . . . working. Clickywidget . . . working. Numplecogs . . .' he whispered, ticking them off in his brain. 'Fluxinator . . . fine . . . Alliotlepops . . .'

His thumb smeared through a patch of sticky oil, following it around the side of the machine. Suddenly, his whole hand sank into a glob of black goo.

'AHA!' he yelled, before yanking out a rather hot, oily carrot.

Instantly, the generator bumped back into life, humming as if nothing had happened.

'It was wounded, by this.' Dev waved the carrot at

Santoro. 'Space Fleet must have found a new monster to attack!'

Santoro grabbed the carrot and turned to the villagers gathering behind them. 'The Guild has fixed the generator. You can all go back to your homes now.'

'But *I* fixed it!' Dev called after him.

'The *Guild* has fixed it,' Santoro insisted, marching back towards the warm, well-lit glow of Middle Eden.

Dev felt his bottom lip start to quiver. After the day he'd had, it was nice to finally do something helpful, and now Santoro wouldn't even let him have that.

It felt unfair.

It felt cruel.

And so Dev did the only thing he could think to do.

He turned away from his brother, and he *ran*.

12
Flemberthyst

No houses had been built up the western side of the mountain, and for good reason. These were the rockier climbs, the crevices and the gullies, weathered by rainfall into deep, perilous drops. Carpeted by great seas of knotted ivy, which spilled down over the lower village like a waterfall.

Even Santoro wouldn't risk scuffing his boots to climb up here.

Dev, however, was already halfway around the rock face by the time his legs gave way. He slumped down on a rocky overhang, clutching his chest, his lungs struggling to find their rhythm again. Tears dripping from his chin.

'Maybe I should just stay here,' he whimpered. 'Out of everyone's way.'

He picked up a rock and flung it as far as he could. It sailed through the air and then down, clattering across a few metal rooftops before disappearing into the streets of Lower Eden.

Someone shouted something. It sounded rude.

Dev sighed.

'Who's up here?' a voice croaked from behind him.

Dev turned to see the glow from a soft, yellow light, and a familiar figure hunched behind it.

'Hi, Nonna,' Dev whispered, wiping the tears from his cheeks. 'Your banana light's still working then?'

'Ah, Dev . . .' Ventillo's huge, magnified eyes peered down at him. She opened up her outer coat to show a multitude of pockets, each one sagging under the weight of spare potatoes. 'I'm on my sixth already. They only work for so long.' Her face cracked into a smile. Then she tilted her head to catch Dev's eye. 'I didn't think anyone else knew about this place.'

Dev looked away. Ventillo shuffled forwards, and

plonked herself beside him.

'I heard about everything that's been going on today,' she said.

'I'm only trying to help.'

'Oh, Dev, you've been telling yourself that since you were young.'

She clasped his hand.

'Such a brilliant brain, but you're *wasting* it. You spend half your time trying to fix your own mistakes. And then trying to fix those mistakes. And those. And then those. You're like a dog chasing its own tail.'

The hairs on the back of Dev's neck bristled. He wasn't quite sure what to make of this. Usually Ventillo was direct, but now there was a frustration in her voice. Perhaps she, too, had finally grown tired of him.

'And stop sulking,' she interrupted, clambering back onto her feet and pulling him up alongside. 'Here, I want to show you something.' Then suddenly she was off, clambering over boulders, tottering along ledges, making her way up the rock face with all the agility, and some of the noises, of a mountain goat.

It surprised Dev. So much so that he could only stumble along behind her.

'This place has always been my little secret,' she smirked. 'Now, I suppose, it's yours too.'

In front of them stood a sheer mountain wall, all but concealed by a thick layer of ivy, which Ventillo pulled apart as if it were a curtain. Behind it, a dark, jagged crack ran up the rock face, just wide enough to climb inside.

And that's exactly what Ventillo did.

Followed, cautiously, by Dev.

It smelt damp in here. It felt cold. The rocks were slippery and, apart from Ventillo's dimly glowing banana, there was no light. By the time Dev's eyes had adjusted, she was already disappearing deeper and deeper into the darkness, walking surprisingly fast for someone weighed down with potatoes.

Dev followed, clonking his helmet on the low, craggy ceiling. They took a sharp left, then a right, sliding down some wet rocks and then taking it in turns to squeeze through a thin opening in the wall.

'Are you ready?' Ventillo whispered, as she popped out the other side.

'For what?' Dev asked as soon as he could breathe out again. He could hear trickling water. Then he could see it, glinting as it ran down the walls in thin strips, then across the ground, disappearing inside a large, dark hole in the middle of the cavern.

Ventillo carefully sat down beside the hole, beckoning for Dev to do the same.

'Have patience,' she said, closing her eyes.

Dev peered around their dimly lit hollow. Listened to the dripping echoes. Watched the breath curl out of his mouth in a fine mist. He shivered. And he was just about to suggest they go home when, suddenly, one of the small rocks in front of him started to glow.

'A flemberthyst!' gasped Dev, scrambling forward to pick it up. 'They're rare!'

As he held it in his hands, the light seemed to fade away.

'That they are.' Ventillo nodded. 'I didn't think anyone else knew about them.'

Dev slid the flemberthyst into his pocket and sat back down. A few moments later, another flemberthyst lit up in front of him. And then another, until soon all the ground around them was flickering.

'The cave is full of flemberthysts!' Dev gasped. 'But they need flember to light them up. Where's it coming from?'

Ventillo pointed towards the hole in front of them. Dev peered inside. He saw water, invisible in the darkness but for its ripples catching the light. Then it churned, and it bubbled, and from within its depths a beautiful white light shone out, racing up the well at speed, spilling out around Dev's feet. The flemberthyst floor lit as brightly as the sun, then up, up the light went, up the walls, spiralling out into a huge, intricate pattern across the ceiling.

'Only happens for a few days every year,' Ventillo whispered. 'Always around Flember Day.'

Small creatures started to skitter out from the dark corners of the cave. Scuttlecrabs, bonklice, hairsnakes. They bathed in the light from the flemberthysts. Tiny lurchershrimp plopped into the water. Bright blue butterflies fluttered across the surface.

Dev held up his arms, his skin prickling with a strange, hazy warmth. 'I've never seen anything like it.'

'It rushes up.' Ventillo mimed. 'In waves, it comes. Can't see it anywhere else on the island but here. Rushes up inside the mountain, right to the top, into the very tips of each branch on the Eden Tree, and

then it all just . . . washes right back down. Back and forth it goes. Back and forth.'

'It's so beautiful!'

'That it is.' Ventillo blinked with contentment. 'I like to imagine your dad's still watching it with me.'

And just then, the rocks began to dim. The insects scuttled away. The glow faded from the water and the cave was plunged back into darkness. Dev could feel a damp chill against his skin.

'We'll see another wave, in a little bit.' Ventillo shrugged.

'Dad came here?'

Ventillo's smile wavered. 'He *found* this place.' She spoke quietly. 'When he was very young. He showed me. Just me. And now, I'm showing you.'

Neither of them said another word. Not for all the time they both sat in the darkness. Not even as wave after wave of flember lit the cave up again. Eventually, Ventillo nudged an elbow into Dev's ribs and together they left. Squeezing back through the thin crack, clambering up the slippery rocks, shuffling along the dark corridors and then out, into the bracing night air.

At which point Ventillo stopped and turned to Dev.

'Flember gives to the village. That's all it does. No fuss, no quarrel, it just gives. You should do the same. Do something *good*. Show them what you're capable of, instead of apologising for all the things you've done wrong.'

In the glow of her banana she reached up, gripping Dev's cheeks between her cold hands.

'Who knows? Maybe they'll invite you back to Flember Day.'

13
An Awful Lot of Bees

It took a little while, and another one and a half potatoes, for Dev and Ventillo to find their way back towards the lights of Middle Eden. Dev bid his grandmother goodnight at the turn in the road, and headed off home. His mind full of flemberthyst-lit memories. His heart singing, happier now than it had been all day.

As soon as his house was in sight, the front door crashed open and his mother came running out and hugged him tightly. Then they walked together into the warmth of the living room. Dev sat at the table while his mother took a whistling kettle from the stove and poured into two misshapen mugs.

'Santoro said you ran off. He's still out looking for you.'

'I was with Nonna.' Dev grabbed a mug with both hands and sipped at it. Heat flushed down his throat. He considered telling his mother all about the flemberthyst cave, how beautiful it was in there, how magical.

But as he looked into her eyes, he realised she wasn't in the mood to hear such things.

'Sorry,' Dev mumbled. 'I didn't mean to worry anyone.'

She turned back to the stove. 'Percy came round too, furious he was. Said you brought Mina into our house. Something about breaking her teddy bear?'

For a brief second, the memory of Boja Bear's screams rang in Dev's ears again. He shuddered.

'From what I gather, it's only Santoro who stopped Percy dragging you back in front of the Mayor. Maybe you should be *thanking* him for that.'

She put a plate of fried duck eggs and toast down in front of him, at which his stomach growled angrily.

Alongside it she slid Dev's jar, still holding Limpy the flemberbug. He was sound asleep, his furry little body heaving up and down with each breath.

Dev smiled affectionately before chomping into a mouthful of egg.

'You're trying your best to make things right, I know that,' she said, watching as he wolfed down great forkfuls of food. 'But this is a quiet village, Dev. People here don't want any fuss, they don't want drama. They just want to feel *safe*. Twelve-year-old boys wearing wings, flying around, spraying cheese, building robots, they don't want all th—'

DINK!

They both heard the noise.

DINK-DINK!

Dev looked up at the network of pipes above his

head, as something *DINK-DINK-DINK-ed* along inside them.

'Pipe B-52,' he yelled, leaping up from his chair.

DINK-DINK-DINK! To the left, to the right. *DINK!* From one pipe into another, then back down again. *DINK-DINK!* Down the wall, into the oven, out through its open door. A single bee *BZZZZZED* right into Dev's cupped hands, tickling his palms as it bobbed around. He walked briskly over to the iron furnace against the wall, kicked open its door and carefully spooned his hands inside.

'Dev, those BEES,' his mother growled with exasperation. 'They're *always* escaping!'

'Bee power is the future!' Dev watched as his bee buzzed around inside, then became lost amongst all the other bees. 'Even a small hive like this gives off *way* more energy than the old generators.'

He stood up, proudly folding his arms. 'One day, everyone will want bees in their house.'

'THERE ARE BEES IN THE HOUSE!' his mother screamed.

Dev had left the door open, and bees were swarming out into the kitchen, billowing like a storm cloud. It took an hour, some saucepans, a curtain and a number of empty jam jars to get all the bees back inside. Dev apologised, apologised again, and then again, but his mother was having none of it.

'Just STOP, Dev.' She lifted off her helmet and slumped down into a chair. 'Maybe everyone's right. Maybe they're all right. I know you're trying to help, but it always just makes things *worse*.'

A chill ran through Dev's bones.

'Just go to bed,' she sighed, burying her head into her hands. 'Please.'

He wasn't sure what to do for a moment. Then he gently slid the stray chairs back under the table, picked up Limpy's jar, made his way towards the back of the house and closed his workshop door very, very slowly. Taking just long enough to see his mother stare up at the picture frame, the one with the painting of her and his father in it. And he thought he saw a tear roll down her cheek.

The door latch closed with a CLUNK.

Dev's workshop was dark and cold, as if it had been abandoned. It felt unwelcoming now. It felt wrong. Apart from the moonlight shining in through the balcony windows, the only other light in here was a faint glow from beneath a pile of engine parts. From the book with the golden F on its cover.

But where this book had once sent a thrill through Dev's chest, now he only remembered Mina crying. Percy furiously trying to get at him. Santoro in the doorway. Smug and bullish as ever.

He stared down at his Makeshift Flember

Transference Device. At the flemberthyst, split into tiny fragments. The whitedrop flower, wilted, its once pillowy petals now grey and brittle.

He carefully picked it up.

'I'm so sorry,' he whispered. 'I took all your flember away for nothing. And I don't know how to put it back.'

He closed his eyes and said a Jikanda prayer, in thanks for the flower's life.

...JIKANDA JOKAY, JIJIN TE SEP...

He carefully placed it back on the bench, and climbed onto his unmade bed, placing Limpy's jar beside him.

'I'll let you out tomorrow,' Dev whispered. 'Then you can fly wherever you like.'

A sad, weak smile crept into the corners of his mouth.

'Wouldn't that be nice.'

His eyes closed, and then he too drifted off to sleep.

14
A Gift

Not long after, Dev was woken by a gentle tapping on his balcony window. At first he ignored it. But when it happened again, and more insistently, he forced himself up to investigate, stepping barefoot onto the wooden boards, shivering in the cold night breeze. He looked from one end to the other and couldn't see anything, but then he caught sight of a round, dark shape resting against the wall. Bigger and wider than him, it was covered with sackcloth, and there was a note attached.

For Dev,
As a thank you for all your hard work.
Perhaps you can make more use of it
than me.
Z

Dev's fingertips ran across the cloth. He could feel ridges beneath it. Delicate little pipes. He pulled at its binding ropes. His brain already knew what was hiding beneath, but his eyes had to see it for themselves.

Zerigauld's golden heart.

In the moonlight it appeared almost ghostly, shimmering and glowing as if it didn't belong in this world. But here it was. Right in front of him. And even more beautiful than he'd remembered.

'Zerigauld wouldn't just give this away,' he started, and then a curious little thought bobbed up into his brain. 'Unless . . . he was worried I might tell someone about the *books*.'

He gasped. 'Zerigauld's buying me off.'

And with that, all his questions and concerns disappeared. All gone in an instant. Immediately replaced by that familiar fire in his belly, the overwhelming lure of discovery.

The many, *many* thoughts of what he could do with a huge, gold heart.

15
Experiment Number 2

'Do something *good*,' Dev
muttered, repeating Ventillo's
advice over and over, as he sat with his
legs dangling over the workshop
balcony. 'Show them what you're
capable of.'

Occasionally, he would turn back
and glance at the gold heart. Just
seeing it fired a bolt of adrenaline
up through his chest, and spread an
uncontrollable grin across his face.

TWANGGGG! Dev's fishing line
pulled tight. He wound its handle

153

until a magnet appeared. Attached to it was a bendy spring, which he carefully inspected, before pulling it off and flinging it onto the pile of bolts, cogs and old engine parts beside him.

The last few hours of scrapyard fishing had been quite a success. Dev stepped inside, dragging the sheet from his bed and laying it across the floor. Then he rolled the pile of scrap across it, before stepping back out for the heart. It was as heavy as you might expect a huge golden heart to be, but he managed to heave it through. With everything in front of him, he tugged on his helmet straps, and all the spotlights and lenses of his Tinkering Helmet folded out in front of his face.

Then he reached up for the flember book, opened it, and started reading the bits he'd skipped before.

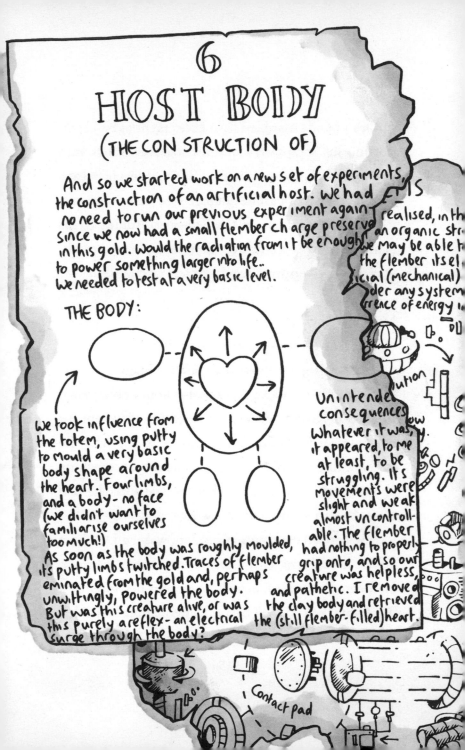

6

HOST BODY

(THE CONSTRUCTION OF)

And so we started work on a new set of experiments, the construction of an artificial host. We had no need to run our previous experiment again since we now had a small flember charge preserved in this gold. Would the radiation from it be enough to power something larger into life.. We needed to test at a very basic level.

...realised, in th
...an organic str
...we may be able t
...the flember itsel
...icial (mechanical)
...der any system
...rrence of energy

THE BODY:

We took influence from the totem, using putty to mould a very basic body shape around the heart. Four limbs, and a body- no face (we didn't want to familiarise ourselves too much!)

As soon as the body was roughly moulded, its putty limbs twitched. Traces of flember eminated from the gold and, perhaps unwittingly, powered the body. But was this creature alive, or was this purely a reflex- an electrical surge through the body?

Unintended consequences
Whatever it was, it appeared, to me at least, to be struggling. It's movements were slight and weak almost uncontrollable. The flember had nothing to properly grip onto, and so our creature was helpless, and pathetic. I removed the clay body and retrieved the (still flember-filled) heart.

Contact pad

Dev's hands trembled with excitement as he began slotting his scrapyard treasures together. Cogs into cogs. Wires between circuits. Springs inside joints. And for each new part he put together, he drew around it, outlining its shape on the bedsheet. Adding to his plans piece by piece by ever more complicated piece.

This time, nothing would be left to chance.

Morning dawned.

24 hours until Flember Day.

24 hours to do something good for Eden.

His mother knocked to say she would be in town till late, helping to decorate the streets. Dev kept his door closed. He didn't want anyone to see what he was working on, not yet, so he mumbled something about feeling unwell, and when he was sure she had gone, he carried on with his work.

She popped back mid-afternoon, waking Dev from an accidental nap with a gentle tapping on the door. He peered out, bleary-eyed, accepting her offer of a Triple-Stacked Bobbleberry Delight from Arnold's

Waffle Shop, before closing the door and dragging a bookcase across it.

No more naps. No more interruptions. He would work on until he was done.

Some hours later, as the cool evening air swooped in over the balcony, Dev finally heaved himself up from his knees. He stepped back to admire what he had built so far.

'You beautiful thing.' He grinned.

Before him stood something for which 'beautiful' might not be the most obvious choice of words. It was a skeleton, of sorts, three times as tall as Dev and maybe five times as wide. Its large metallic ribcage held all manner of canvas sacks, engine parts and circuitry, and it was flanked by four sturdy limbs, each stuffed with various pistons and bellows. Next to this body, a 'head' lay on the floor.

Two bulbous eyes staring out from a mesh of wires and flashing lights. A rubbery tongue lolling out of its huge mouth.

And yet, it all still needed a heart.

Dev rested a ladder against the skeleton. Step by wobbly step, he heaved the golden heart up towards its open neck, before carefully lowering it down inside. It sank into thick, shiny goo, nestling in front of a bulging set of lungs.

He wired it in.

Getting there.

The head next. Again, a struggle to lift but eventually it settled into place. All wires and pipes connected. All bolts bolted.

Nearly done.

Now, skin.

He mixed pink putty together with gum from the spindletrees until it became like clay. Hard enough to hold, but still

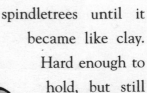

flexible. He slathered it across the skeleton in big dollops. Then, fur. Bright-red, thick fur, unravelled from a huge roll he kept tucked up in the rafters, and stitched, inch by inch, into the hardening clay.

After some time, Dev twisted his helmet lamps up, and leant back on his weary, clay-covered arms.

'I think . . . you're finally *done*!'

He stared up at his most ambitious invention yet. A five-metre tall robot, as red as a bobbleberry, as furry as a snarklecub. With short, dumpy legs, thick, strong arms, a big, black, glistening nose and two furry ears, which nearly skimmed the ceiling.

'You'll keep *everyone* safe.' Dev smiled, flinging his last chunk of lunchtime waffle into the robot's open mouth. 'Won't you, Boja Bear?'

INVENTION 501: Boja Bear

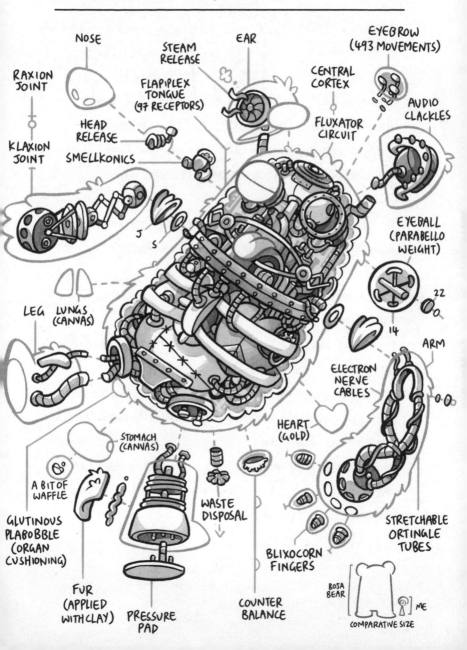

RAXION JOINT

KLAXION JOINT

NOSE

HEAD RELEASE

SMELLKONICS

STEAM RELEASE

FLAPIPLEX TONGUE (97 RECEPTORS)

EAR

CENTRAL CORTEX

FLUXATOR CIRCUIT

EYEBROW (493 MOVEMENTS)

AUDIO CLACKLES

J

S

EYEBALL (PARABELLO WEIGHT)

22

14

LEG

LUNGS (CANVAS)

ARM

ELECTRON NERVE CABLES

HEART (GOLD)

A BIT OF WAFFLE

GLUTINOUS PLABOBBLE (ORGAN CUSHIONING)

STOMACH (CANVAS)

WASTE DISPOSAL

STRETCHABLE ORTINGLE TUBES

BLIXOCORN FINGERS

FUR (APPLIED WITH CLAY)

PRESSURE PAD

COUNTER BALANCE

BOJA BEAR

ME

COMPARATIVE SIZE

16
Just a Spoonful

Limpy the flemberbug was stirring inside his jar.
Rubbing his little legs together to make a sound.
CLIK. CLIK-CLIK.

Flember Day would soon be dawning. Flemberbugs
just knew.

'I was supposed to let you out!' Dev yelped,
tilted the jar and twisted off its lid. Limpy slid down
inside the glass and plopped onto the floor. He staggered a little. His wonky leg trailed behind him.
He fluttered his wings, cleaned his antennae, then
looked up at Dev with a sweet, inquisitive stare. Dev
smiled and offered his hand, but Limpy had already
fluttered up and away from him.

Heading for the window, bonking into the window frame.

And then, on his second try, he flew out into the night sky.

'Now! Back to the task at hand.' Dev grinned, jumping up onto his bed and pulling down all the cables from his ceiling. One by one they *PINGED* from their bolts, uncurling like snakes from around the rafters. He wrapped them over his shoulder in huge rings, picked up a handful of clamps and then stepped out onto the balcony, climbing over the railings and into the bracken beside the house.

He knelt down in the darkness, clamping one of the cables around the stalk of a whuppleberry bush. The next he embedded into the spiky bark of a spindletree, and the next he wrapped around a large clump of heather.

'When the flowers are in their fullest bloom.' Dev imitated the Mayor's pompous voice. 'The grass is at its tallest, the trees are *humming* with life . . . well

that's why Flember Day is the perfect time for me to borrow a bit of flember. If I take just a drop, from a few different plants, then it won't be like what happened with the whitedrop at *all*. I bet it won't even be missed.'

Dev trailed the cables over his balcony and back into his workshop. He reached into his pocket, pulled out the flemberthyst crystal from the cave, slathered it with what was left of his clay, and stuck the end of each cable into it. Then he climbed the stepladder up to Boja Bear's face and wedged the whole sticky ball between the glistening white marble teeth.

He looked down at the schematics on his bedsheet and ran through every connection in his mind. Then ran through them all again. Then he re-read the flember book, all the way through, right up to the last page.

Dev flipped the page back and forth, holding it up to the light, peering closely to find anything that might be written upon it.

But nothing. From here he was on his own.

He took a deep, deep breath.

'Like taking a spoonful of water from a lake,' he muttered, yanking the handle from the top of the birdcage, wedging it up into Boja's right nostril, and turning it.

Inside its sticky cocoon, the flemberthyst began to hum. Quietly, at first. Then louder. And louder. The cables spilling out from Boja's mouth writhed around, dancing across the floor, little pinpricks of blue light peeping out of them.

Flember!

Suddenly, the lights turned into lightning bolts, jumping from cable to cable. A deafening buzz filled the workshop – it jangled the jars on the walls and set everything inside them writhing and tapping against the glass. The air itself felt hazy and alive. Dev's clothes crackled with static and his scarf rose like a nettlesnake.

'UHHHH . . .'

It came from deep within Boja Bear, a groan that only made Dev grip the handle tighter, and spin it even faster.

'UHHHHHHHH . . .'

The bear's eyes remained closed. A sweet smell wafted out between his clenched teeth. Dev could see a faint glow coming from inside Boja's other nostril and then, to Dev's delight, droplets of bright blue light crackled across his fur.

'B-Boja Bear?' Dev said.

'BBBBBBBBBB . . .'

Dev spun the handle faster, and faster, as fast as his arms could manage.

And the faster he went, the brighter Boja Bear glowed, until the

whole workshop, from floor to rafters, was bathed in light. Boja Bear's chest heaved up and down in long, laboured breaths until suddenly . . .

Doompf.

The heart!

Doompf!

Doompf!

Boja Bear's eyelids lifted to reveal huge, bulging white eyes. Dev let go of the handle but it continued to spin. Faster. And *fasterrrrr*. Blue light crackled out from Boja Bear's fur in great blinding arcs. It blasted across the walls, carving through Dev's workbench, his experiments, shattering through his specimen jars. He stumbled down from the ladder and hid behind a crate, peeking out just long enough to see Boja Bear's teeth *CHOMP* down on the flemberthyst, shattering it into a thousand pieces.

Utterly consuming him in light.

Then everything exploded.

17
Boja Bear

After what felt like a very long time, but was possibly just a few seconds, Dev unscrunched his eyes. He poked his head out from behind the crate. The only heartbeat he could hear now was his own, hammering loudly in his ears.

He peered through the smoke. Everything he owned looked smashed or blackened, every shelf and cabinet had collapsed. The walls were thick with soot, and the roof was half destroyed, allowing a faint beam of early dawn light to shine down upon Boja Bear.

Boja Bear!

There he stood, in the middle of the room. His fur

sparkling with bright blue lights. The handle up his nose slowly spinning to a halt.

Flember flooded up inside his eyeballs, and Dev could see they were staring straight back at him.

'B-Boja Bear?'

Boja Bear moaned again.

Dev stepped across the shredded cables, through the dust and the debris, unable to take his eyes off the big glowing bear in front of him. He reached a finger out towards his belly. Blue sparks span out from the fur, across his hand, and threaded up his arm.

It felt good.

It felt warm.

'You're *full* of flember,' Dev gasped, standing on tiptoe to reach Boja Bear's nose. He gently pulled the handle out, wiping a few drips of sparkling blue snot from his nostrils. 'How are you feeling?'

Boja Bear slowly lifted an arm and waggled his fingers. Then he did the same with the other, as if he were playing an imaginary piano.

A strange, distorted giggle rose up from his throat.

'Boja Bear.' Dev stared at Boja Bear's paws with just as much amazement. 'That's your name. *Boja* for short.'

'Boh . . .' Boja began. 'Bohhhhhhhhh . . .'

His mouth seemed to get stuck on the word.

'I'm Dev.' Dev gently lifted Boja's paw, and placed it on his own head. 'Me. I'm Dev.'

Boja patted Dev's head. 'Dvvvvvv.'

'That'll do.' Dev could feel the contented *thump-thump-thump* of Boja's pulse. 'I *made* you, Boja.'

Boja's gaze flickered over Dev's shoulder. To the

sky beyond his balcony, and the faintest glimmers of an orange sun. He reached out towards it.

'It's morning.' Dev smiled. 'That's the sun!'

'Snnnnn,' Boja repeated, dragging a heavy foot forward with a loud *THUD*. The other foot followed, and before Dev knew what was happening, Boja was marching his huge lumbering body towards the balcony.

'SNNNN!'

'Boja, NO!' Dev shouted.

The doorway was too small for the giant bear to fit through, but his wobbly legs had already committed to this ridiculous plan, and there was no pulling out now. Under his weight the whole wall crumbled like wet cardboard, wrenching the entire back half of the workshop into the misty dawn sky.

'BOJA!' Dev screamed, the floorboards tearing away beneath the bear's feet. Dev could only watch in horror as his creation, his amazing, magical creation, tumbled down the rock face, disappearing into great billows of dust.

Landing on a pile of scrap far, far below.

His eyes closed.

His glowing body utterly motionless.

18
Preparations

There was a loud hammering against the workshop door. Santoro shouted from behind it, something angry. Something muffled. Dev knew he only had a few seconds to spare. He scrambled across the room, searching through the rubble for the flember book, but it was nowhere to be seen.

'What did you DO?' Santoro yelled, barging the door open with one hefty push. He climbed over the bookcase, yanking hard on Dev's scarf, dragging him through the house, and out onto the front lawn. Their mother was there, her helmet decorated with antlers and clumps of moss. Her eyes glistening with tears.

'You're OK.' She winced a smile.

'I was . . . trying to extract the saliva from . . . f-f-f-flutterskit moths,' Dev stammered. 'Very explosive, flutterskits. They only have to lean the wrong way, and . . . BOOM!'

She wasn't buying it.

'I'm sorry.' Dev sighed, an uncomfortable lump rising up inside his throat. 'I'm really, really sorry.'

He waited for his mother to do that thing. That thing where she'd clench her jaw, scrunch up her nose and let out a long, frustrated growl. *Do stop blowing things up*, she'd say, and then she'd hug him.

But nothing came. No scrunched up nose, no growl. No sigh. No hug.

Just a blank stare.

'We'll be late for Flember Day,' she finally said.

Santoro's face fell like a giant robot bear tumbling down a mountainside. 'Dev's not coming to Flember Day. No way!'

The thought didn't much appeal to Dev, either. Not while Boja Bear was lying unconscious on a pile of scrap. 'Santoro's right, Mum. I'll stay here. I'll . . . I'll fix the house! I'll rebuild the workshop. I'll have it all perfect again by nightfall! You go!'

'YOU'RE COMING WITH US,' she snapped, making both Dev and Santoro jump. Then she took a deep breath and composed herself. 'Flember Day is important. To me, it's important.' She shot a furious glance at Dev. 'And I'll not spend it worrying what else you're blowing up.'

'He's not coming.' Santoro folded his arms across his tunic. 'The Mayor banned him. The Guild would arrest him on sight.'

'The Guild won't see him.' She reached inside the front door and pulled a long brown cloak from the coat rack. She wrapped it around Dev's upper half, tighter than a cocooned woodgrub, concealing all but his eyes.

'There.' She smiled, sticking twigs into the folds and hanging vines between them.

'Us nffpm verr cmmfabull,' Dev mumbled.

'Well, Dev, that's the price you pay for destroying half our house. We're going to Flember Day, all of us, as a family, and you'll both just have to deal with it.'

Dev poked his nose above the cloak, breathing in the crisp air as he, Santoro and their mother followed a trail of flickering lanterns towards the marketplace. Although it was still ridiculously early in the morning, there was plenty of activity.

Villagers pegged the marquees, laid out the tables and prepared food for the banquets. Everyone wearing and comparing their own decorated helmets – each adorned with all manner of horns and antlers, vines and leaves, mushrooms, flowers and berries. Some had smeared their clothes with moss, others had insects scuttling across their shoulders, in and out of their sleeves, up and down their trousers.

A cry came from over the hill. 'Out of the way! Mind! Mind out of my way!'

Dev saw sparklers sticking out from an almighty mound of bobbleberries and cream, dolloped on stack, upon stack of giant waffles. All wobbling from side to side as Arnold the waffle maker pushed it along on a large cart.

His pride and joy. His Flember Day Special.

The villagers chattered excitedly.

'Oh don't encourage him,' Nomilie, Arnold's wife, grumbled. 'He's been obsessed with that awful waffle. OBSESSED! We've barely seen him for weeks!'

The two children who had been clinging to her dress suddenly broke free, running over to their father. Arnold tutted and fussed, trying to keep their stumpy little fingers from dipping in the cream. Santoro stepped forwards to help, and Dev took the opportunity to slowly, slyly back away into the hustle and bustle of the crowd.

'Are you in disguise?' Commander Sam of Space Fleet bumped alongside him. His helmet was now painted with mud, decorated with little blue lights, and he wore what looked like an entire hedge as a costume. Beside him stood Reginald who, for reasons best known to himself, was dressed like a pig.

'You recognised me!' Dev grinned. 'I should have known you would. Well, yes, actually I *am* in disguise. I'm . . . I'm on a secret mission!'

'Ooh! Ooh! What's the mission?' Sam giggled.

Reginald oinked.

'Well . . . I left something behind . . . in Percy's Scrapyard,' Dev whispered. 'So I need to sneak back there without anyone seeing me!'

He shrank down inside his cloak, staring out at the crowd. 'I need a distraction!'

Sam thought for a moment, then pushed Reginald onto the ground. 'REGINALD'S FARTING!' he shrieked as Reginald rolled around, crumpling up his pig outfit, making loud oinky farting noises with his mouth.

'I – *FRRP!* – drank some hibbicus beer! *Oink!*' he moaned. 'MY TUMMY – *FRRPPP! OINK!* – IT'S GOING TO EXPLODE!'

The crowd gasped, some laughed, the sensible ones backed away. Sam winked at Dev. The mission was a *go*.

The mission was not a go.

Amy gripped Dev's wrist just as he was about to move. 'Don't you dare,' she hissed.

'Amy!' Bastor stepped out in front of them both, his weathered cheeks blushing a delicate blossom pink.

Dev caught his eye for just a second before nestling deeper down inside his coat and shuffling behind his mother. Her hand slipped from his. The farting pig hadn't worked as a distraction, but a flustered Bastor had.

'D-did you hear the thunder this morning?' Bastor continued. 'Huge crack of noise it was. Rumbled right through the village.'

'Oh really?' She nervously smiled in reply. 'I must

have slept right through it.'

Bastor chuckled uncomfortably, grinning inanely at her.

'Well, it's been nice to see you, Bastor.'

'Oh!' Bastor reached into his tunic, pulling out the silver heart. 'I meant to show you, back in the forge. I made this. For you.'

As Bastor stuttered and giggled, Dev was busy hiding himself behind the Flember Day Special. From here he could plan out the clearest path home.

Fervus the goat, however, had other ideas.

'Fervus!' Dev hissed, nudging the goat away with his foot. 'Stop chewing my cloak!'

'Fervus?' Bastor leant around the giant waffle. 'And . . . DEV? You're not allowed anywhere near Flember Day, Dev. You know that. By order of the Mayor.'

Dev's mouth opened and closed, until finally some words fell out.

'Where's Mum?'

'Looking for you, I suspect,' Bastor snorted.

'Did she like the heart?'

Bastor's shoulders slumped. 'She said it was nice,' he sighed. 'Just . . . nice. Walked off before I could give it to her.'

'I mean, it is nice.' Dev reached up and pulled one of the thinner vines from his cloak, biting it down to a more manageable length. He took the silver heart

 from between Bastor's fingers, wrapped the vine three times around it and held

it up as a necklace.

'But now it's *useful*.'

Bastor was silent for a few moments, before tucking the necklace back inside his tunic. The smallest of smiles crept up beneath his beard. 'If you must be here, just keep out of sight, OK?' He scooped Fervus up and tucked him under his arm, walking away with a surprisingly light spring in his step.

Dev thumbed a splodge of cream from the Flember Day Special into his mouth. 'Feels good to help.' He smiled, a moment of cheer that lasted approximately three seconds.

'My 'EART!' Zerigauld clung to his shop doorway. 'Someone's stolen me gold 'EART!'

19
The Parade

The Guild huddled around Zerigauld, but they couldn't keep him quiet, couldn't stop him screaming about the theft of his golden heart.

'I was only closed for one day! They must 'ave known! Must 'ave snuck in while I was at me sister's! Don't tell *me* to keep quiet! I've been thieverised! Someone 'ere thieverised me right up!'

Dev watched, his mouth agape, his thoughts only broken when Santoro's hand slapped down upon his shoulder.

'So, what did you do with it?' Santoro smirked.

Dev could only squeak.

'Oh come on. Zerigauld's heart.' Santoro nudged

him in the ribs. 'I saw you had your eye on it.'

'I . . . I didn't . . . ' Dev went a deathly pale, as if all of his blood was draining from his body. 'Zerigauld left it for me on my balcony. To say thank you for all the cleaning I did.'

Santoro tried to stifle a laugh until it was too much to hold in. 'You . . . you thought it was from *him*? Zerigauld? That wrinkly old bag of bones? Dev, he hates you! He hates everyone! Why on earth would he ever give you his prized gold heart?'

Dev mouthed a response, but even he didn't know what he was trying to say.

'*I* took the heart, Dev. And *I* left it on your balcony,' Santoro hissed into his ear. 'I thought that supposedly brilliant brain of yours would realise it was a joke. A set-up. Then you'd panic, and try to sneak the heart back into his shop. Probably get caught doing it.' Santoro leant in close and winked. 'Probably get caught by me.'

The words didn't quite fit together in Dev's brain. 'You . . . *you* stole the heart?'

'Yes. I. Stole. It.'
Santoro playfully snapped
a twig from Dev's helmet
with each word.
'Then you *planted* it . . .
on me?' Dev growled.

'Give it back to Zerigauld, if you don't want it.'
Santoro grinned.

Even though his brother stood a few inches taller,
and was armed with a rather large sword, Dev felt a
rising urge to lunge at him. To topple him down onto
the ground, knocking that huge, smug smile from his
face. Demanding to know why – why his own brother
was always so mean to him, why he'd go *this far* to
make Dev look bad.

'Whatever you two are arguing about,' their
mother slid between them, 'do NOT do it here. And
NOT today.'

Dev unclenched a fist he hadn't realised he was
making.

'Are we here? ARE WE ALL HERE?' The Mayor's

ridiculous, oversized helmet bobbed through the crowds. Guild members marched alongside, each holding tall flagpoles, their blue flags fluttering in the breeze.

'Fifty-two minutes.' The Mayor stared at his clock. 'Fifty-two minutes exactly. Oh! Fifty-one! Ladies and gentlemen of Eden, I'll make this swift, we're already one minute behind. It looks like a beautiful morning is set to dawn, etcetera, etcetera, and so on, and so on. IN CONCLUSION, if you would all care to follow me, we will make our way up to the Eden Tree for today's thanksgivings.' The Mayor lolloped forwards, a procession of bizarrely dressed villagers shuffling along behind him.

'SWIFTLY,' he shouted, and they quickened their step.

Before Dev could say another word to Santoro, he felt a push from his mother and then he too was part of the crowd, jostled and swept along like a ship on the waves. They marched from the marketplace into the hills, swapping the stone buildings of Middle

Eden for the towering trees of the Old Woods. Everything had been carefully prepared to look as pleasing as possible to the Mayor's eye. The path was swept clear of twigs, some of the shrubs manicured into a variety of animals, and the most symmetrical moss-covered rocks and boulders were rolled out to line the route.

'What a beautiful village we are blessed with,' the Mayor sighed, as a confused din of bugles and trumpets sounded from within the parade. 'What

riches nature gives us.'

The climb steepened as they headed towards the rice fields. The path became muddier and more slippery. Mayor Bumblebuss clambered onto Bastor's back to keep his feet dry. The rest of the Guild fell back to help lift Arnold's waffle cart, sinking into the ground as they did. Arnold shouted and panicked and rushed around, trying to catch any stray splodges of cream.

A small group of farmers, standing knee-deep

in the perfectly still paddies of water, looked on in amusement.

'We can't carpet this bit?' The Mayor snorted, kicking his heels into Bastor's ribs. 'My mayoral robes are getting filthy.'

Dev stopped to catch his breath. He looked back over the long line of people behind them, trailing back through the Old Woods, back, even, into the marketplace. He looked towards the scrapyard, to where his great big robot bear was lying. Or at least, he hoped it still was. Perhaps it had woken up again and wandered off. Or someone had found it. Perhaps *Percy* had found it. Perhaps Percy was tearing it apart for scrap right now.

Sweat began to prickle up beneath the many layers of Dev's cloak. To his relief, he spotted Percy in the procession, some way behind. His face scrunched up like an old lady's elbow. His mouth puckering like a cat's bum. Beside him walked Mina, her helmet consumed by a giant mushroom cap, her blue bunches bobbing along beneath it, a huge grin across her face

194

as she waggled a flag in her bandaged hand.

Dev raised his arm to wave, but his mother lowered it back down.

'You're not supposed to be here, remember?'

They continued along the muddy path, through paddocks and cornfields, up between rocky crevices, until finally, *finally*, Dev stepped through the first bending willows of Shady Acres. Up here it felt like a different world. The grass was thicker, the trees taller. The air fresher. Up here grew things not seen anywhere else on the mountain, such as the dew-covered bilderdrops, lumpy, green pojoboplants and giant orange jimona flowers. Dev marvelled at the glowing algae across the ponds, at the blue and green glow-worms nesting in the tree hollows. At the hum and the warmth and the abundance of it all.

'Ahh, we're here.' Ventillo shuffled along beside Dev, plomping herself down on the grass and blinking up into the sky. 'Now everyone be quiet, if you don't mind.'

A droning noise sounded in the distance. It

came from way, way down the mountain, beyond The Wall, out from the darkness of the surrounding island. A drone that grew louder, and louder. And louder. Something *CLIK-CLIK-CLIKKED* past Dev's ear. Then something else. Then the drone was above them, as loud as their ears could bear. Dev looked up to see a swarm – no, a tidal wave – of insects filling the sky.

Rather *chubby* insects.

'FLEMBERBUGS!' he cheered.

'Therrrrre they are,' Ventillo sighed, her face crinkling up with a wide, enchanted smile.

'BANG ON TIME!' The Mayor lifted his clock with one hand, and fist-pumped with the other. 'From all over the island, regular as clockwork.'

The crowd cheered and ran beneath the flemberbugs, trying to keep up with them, out from the shadow of the trees and taking huge strides up the grass-covered steps.

Until there it was.

The Eden Tree.

Spiralling higher than anything else on the whole island. So high, Dev couldn't even see the top of it. Its trunk as wide as a street of houses. Its long,

knotted arms holding out great clumps of vibrant green leaves, which bustled and swayed in the early-morning breeze. And into this rich foliage flew the flemberbugs. Clamping onto the bark, their furry bottoms bobbing up and down as they jostled for space. They fed from the tree, basking in its flember, glowing bright blue as it filled their bodies. Tiny little dots alighting one by one, until soon the whole Eden Tree was shining with the most beautiful blue light.

'Flember.' Dev gazed wistfully at the sight of it.

'FLEMBER!' The Mayor barged past him. 'As before, so it continues. The annual migration of the flemberbugs. To suck at the nectar of our Eden Tree. Reminding us all, I'm sure, of the—'

'THEY'RE DYING!' Percy shouted.

The lights were flickering out. Flemberbugs tumbled away from the trunk, bouncing lifelessly down onto the ground. The Eden Tree itself, so mighty and impressive only seconds ago, appeared to stiffen, curling its branches in on itself.

'It's all . . . DYING!'

20
The Charge

All Dev could do was watch as the Eden Tree's leaves turned brown and crisp, catching on the wind and spinning out to sea. The trunk splintered, its bark cracking, its rich layers of moss crinkling up into a dusty ash.

'Our . . . TREE!' the Mayor gasped.

'Not just the tree!' Rosa Mildew pointed to the ground beneath their feet. Where grass had grown just moments ago, now it was grey and brittle. The bilderdrops and pojoboplants were wilting. The jimona flowers collapsed, their once fluorescent orange petals shrivelling up like old balloons.

'All our flember's disappearing!' came a voice.

'Save what you can!' came another.

The crowd scattered, picking at flowers, glow-worms, anything which might still hold some flember. Some chased after the few surviving flemberbugs, others tumbled into the quickly drying-up ponds and scooped out great armfuls of algae. They competed, and they fought. They snarled and they snatched. It only took a few minutes, but fear swiftly turned the villagers into a mob.

The Guild's calls for order were ignored, and they were left with little choice but to go in swinging. Bastor CLONK-CLONK-CLONKED the hilt of his sword across a number of decorated helmets, while Rosa Mildew had a villager headlocked under each arm. Which, if you'd ever smelt under her arms, was perhaps the cruellest punishment of all.

'It's heading towards the crops!' screeched the Mayor, who had been lifted out of harm's way and was now crowd surfing across everyone's heads, bobbing up and down in a furious display of limbs.

'Our village is *doomed*!'

The cloak slipped from Dev's head as he looked around. 'This shouldn't be happening,' he mumbled. 'This really, really shouldn't be happening.'

'I KNEW IT!' Someone pushed Dev and sent him crashing to the ground. Instantly, Zerigauld Sourface was upon him, his boot on his helmet like a hawk holding its prey. 'I KNEW you'd sneak up 'ere.'

Dev tried to reply, but Zerigauld's boot just pressed down harder.

'*Everdew.*' His tongue curled around the name.

THUMP!

'Funny 'ow things go wrong when yous . . .'

THUMP!

His voice trailed off.

THUMP!

Dirt rattled across the ground.

THUMP!

THUMP!

THUMP!

THUMP THUMP THUMP!

Then through a multitude of legs, Dev saw it. A huge shadow, swathed in the most brilliant, beautiful blue light. Its paws slamming into the ground as it galloped through Shady Acres.

THUMP! THUMP! THUMP!

'HOOOARGHHHHHH!'

Boja! Those huge eyes, blazing with light. That tongue flapping wildly from his mouth. That big shiny nose, twitching furiously, as if pulling him onwards.

And to the left.

Wayyyy over to the left.

Boja ploughed through the mob, sending a variety of decorated helmets spinning up into the air. He only stopped when he tripped and collapsed onto his own face, but within seconds he'd rolled upright again, tottering onto his unsteady legs. His nose twitched and he turned, first staggering, then running, towards Dev and Zerigauld. He tried to leap over them but grossly misjudged and with a loud *SQUARK* Zerigauld was gone, bundled into the sky by the bear, a long line of flember trailing behind

them both. Zerigauld's pale, wrinkly legs waggling out from beneath Boja's fur.

Everything seemed to move in slow motion.

Then Boja landed in the crater of a dried-out pond, and the whole mountain shook under his weight.

'Boja!' Dev slid down into the mud, struggling to touch Boja's fur for all the flember crackling across it. 'Can you hear me?'

'UHHHHHHH . . .' Boja's eyes spun around in their sockets.

'Boja, it's me! It's Dev! Remember, from the workshop?'

'DDVVVVV . . .' Boja grinned. One of his eyes locked onto Dev.

'Dev! That's right!' Dev whooped with joy. 'Did you . . . did you come all the way up here to find me?'

Boja's shiny black nose started to twitch again. He sniffed at the breeze. His tongue smacked inside his mouth and then, within an instant, he was up and out of the pond, all arms and legs, staggering wildly through the crowds. Swerving left and right, as if being dragged along an invisible trail.

A trail that ended at Arnold's Flember Day Special.

The horror of what was about to happen spread across Arnold's face. He leapt in front of his cart, his eyes wide.

'N-N-N-NO!' he yelped. 'It's mine! IT'S MINE!'

The waffle maker held his nerve as long as he could, but at the last moment he leapt out of the way, and with an almighty *SPLUTCH*, Boja slammed himself face-first into the giant stack of waffles. Once or twice he hauled his head out for air, before chomping back down on great mouthfuls of whipped cream and bobbleberries. Then he rolled onto his back, closed his eyes and sucked waffle bits from his fingers.

'MINE!' He beamed.

Dev pushed through the surrounding crowd. 'His first word!'

'Mine!' Boja repeated, nestling his buttocks deeper into the cream. 'Mine, mine, mine, mine!'

A few Guild members stepped forward, their swords drawn towards Boja.

'No, no. It's OK.' Dev held up his hands. 'He must have followed the waffles up here! I'll pay for it, I will!'

'WOHHHH-FFFFFLES!' Boja garbled.

An excited chuckle rose up from inside Dev's chest. 'He's called Boja,' he said proudly. 'I *made* him!'

The Mayor, who until now had been crouched behind Bastor, peeked out. 'You did . . . what?'

'I made him. I mean, I . . . *invented* him.' Dev caught sight of his mother's face in the crowd. She looked stunned.

They all looked stunned.

'From old parts. I put him together, like a robot. And then I, well, I sort of . . . brought him to *life*.'

'Now, Dev. Be sensible.' Bastor kept his sword firmly trained on Boja. 'You make toys and contraptions. Little, whirry, flappy things. The clanking and the fizzling. You know? That's what you do. But this is a . . . well, it's . . .'

He puffed out his cheeks. 'I mean. What *is* it?'

'His name is *Boja*,' Dev repeated. 'I thought he could help. Any time anything goes wrong, Boja can protect us. He could stop a rampaging Washtopus just by standing in its way, then he could help clean up the mess! Look how big he is, how strong.'

'You built that thing –' the Mayor raised an eyebrow '– to protect us from *you*?'

'N . . . no! Well, a bit. But not just me. He could hold back rockslides, lift whole buildings. When the fields need digging he could do it with his great big paws.' Dev emphasised each point by miming it. 'He's a force for good, a great big *guardian*! He'll keep the whole village safe!'

No one responded. His heart sank a little.

'I thought you'd be pleased.'

A flemberbug stirred beside Boja. Up until now it had been lying on its back, legs folded in towards its belly, half-buried in waffle syrup. But it flipped, and it flopped, and it rolled around in the dirt, before fluttering up and landing on the bear's big black nose. Glowing as it padded back and forth between his eyes.

Another flemberbug landed on Boja's belly and it, too, started to glow. A shiny green flutterskit moth landed on his toes. A jibbernywick landed on his ear, and soon all manner of insects were hovering around him. Basking in his beautiful blue light.

'He's incredible.' Ventillo Everdew pushed to the front of the crowd, utterly entranced by the big, glowing bear. She wrapped her thin fingers around Dev's hand, and squeezed it tightly.

'You both are.'

21
The Everdews

'I t's a MONSTER!' Zerigauld hauled himself out from the crater. His wooden nose was  halfway around his face. 'It attacked me. You saw it! You all did! I'm – *hack!* – I'm lucky to be alive – *haaack!*'

He fell down to his knees, lurching back and forth, before coughing up a big red hairball. Then he staggered back onto his feet, grabbed a clump of dirt and flung it towards Boja. Boja barely reacted. Nor at the second clump.

Nor the third.

Boja was enjoying waffles.

'Look at what it's doing,' Bastor gasped. He pointed his sword down towards Boja's bottom, beneath which lush, green grass was now growing, its dew shimmering with flember. Tiny glowing mushrooms popped up – *Plink! Plink! Plink!* – along with daisies, redbells and drooping spotted whistleflutes.

The Mayor's whole face – jowls, eyebags and all – sank down towards his neck ruffles. 'Flember,' he gasped. 'Right before our very eyes!'

He raised his eyes slowly from Boja's buttocks all the way up to his face. 'This thing . . . it's full of *flember*. Did it . . . did it take OURS?'

Dev suddenly went very, very pale. Somewhere in his mind he'd already made the connection, but he'd been so excited about Boja's appearance he'd barely had a chance to process it. 'I . . . I . . .' He stammered, his throat croaking for air. 'I may have *borrowed* a little flember, just a little, just enough to . . .'

Whichever way he looked, the arched, dead Eden Tree was always in view.

'I didn't mean to take so much.'

He turned to the crowd, who all stared back in disbelief.

'It brought Boja to *life*,' Dev whimpered.

'So is that what you needed the heart for?' Santoro's voice rose from amongst the Guild. 'Is it inside that thing?'

"EART?' Zerigauld shrieked, so high-pitched it was barely audible. 'What 'eart? MY 'eart?'

Zerigauld rushed for
Dev, grabbing him by
his scarf. 'You THIEF!'
he spat. 'You callous,
lying little thief!'

'I . . . didn't . . .' Dev choked.

'Leave him ALONE!' Dev's mother broke from
the crowd, grabbing Zerigauld's arms and struggling
to pull him away. 'Get your hands off my son!'

''E's a GOBBLETOAD!' Zerigauld shouted. 'A
purple-nosed weasel! A rotten, stinking f-f-footface!'

'Santoro!' Dev gasped. 'Santoro took your heart.'

Zerigauld dropped him on the ground, then
blinked furiously at Santoro.

'Your brother? Your fine, upstanding brother?
Pride of the Youth Guild? Future Guild Leader in
waiting? Yerrr . . . brother? Hear that, Amy? Yer boy,
Dev. Trying to ruin his brother's reputation, jus' to
save 'imself.'

'He *did* steal it,' Dev mumbled.

Zerigauld lunged for him again, but this time he

didn't even get close. Boja's arm swung out, lifting Zerigauld off his feet and propelling him across the novelty helmets of the crowd. Far, far into the distance, until he landed with a *squark* in a bustle of crunchy ferns.

Everyone was silent. Apart from Ventillo, who was laughing.

The Mayor's chins wobbled with rage. 'Guild! Seize that . . . that THING! I don't know what's going on here, but I know that BEAST had something to do with it!'

Dev ran in front of Boja. 'It's not his fault! Don't hurt him!'

'Seize Dev too!' the Mayor barked. 'We'll try him for his crimes!'

'JUST YOU TRY IT!' Ventillo picked up a branch and swung it wildly towards the Guild. 'We Everdews don't go down easy!'

'AND HER!' The Mayor's face looked like it might burst. 'AND AMY. AND SANTORO. ARREST THE WHOLE BLINKING FAMILY!'

'You can't arrest me. I'm GUILD!' Santoro protested, but the Guild had already turned their swords on him. Santoro unsheathed his own, swinging it back towards them, growling like a cornered fox. A few of the Guild panicked, and lifted their swords back towards Boja. He growled too, a growl so low it rattled around in his lung sacks, rumbling though his metal bones, igniting his flember as if he were on fire.

Then the Guild turned on Amy.

Dev watched through wide, horrified eyes, his heart pounding, his legs shaking. He started towards his mother, but she stopped him in his tracks with a hard stare.

'We can fend for ourselves,' she said, elbowing a Guild member in the nose. 'But you, you need to run.'

She nodded at Boja.

'You both do.'

Dev stepped back towards Boja, gripping his fur as if it was all he had to hold onto.

'Dev, RUN!' His mother shouted.

Dev turned to Boja, grabbing his cheeks so they squished up his face, and he stared into the bear's glowing blue eyes.

'Boja, run,' he whispered.

22
Flight

Dev could hear the golden heart inside Boja's chest. It was thumping harder now, and faster, clattering against his internal mechanics. Boja slid an arm around Dev's waist, hauling him up onto his back, and with an almighty roar he lunged forward. Through the swords. Through the crowd. Away from Shady Acres and down the rock face, through the withering stalks of the cornfield, across the cracked mud plains of the rice paddies and into the Old Woods.

And out of the woods.

Across the marketplace. The tables and tents didn't stand a chance against Boja's stampede as food and drink was flung into the air around him. He caught a ham joint in his mouth, swallowed it whole and grinned at Dev.

'THIS IS MINE!'

'Sentences?'
Dev laughed. Despite
everything else, he couldn't
help delighting in his creation.
'Boja, your brain circuits, they're learning so
FAST!'

Boja responded with the biggest, ugliest belch Dev

had ever been downwind of. It wobbled his whole face, flecks of spit and ham splattering down onto Dev's helmet. It was only drowned out by a louder sound; a huge, terrifying sound, the sound of the earth tearing itself apart as a wide crack opened up in the ground. It threw Boja off balance. He clipped the corner of Zerigauld's antique shop, ricocheting across the street like a pinball.

SMASH! THUMP! CRASH!

Back and forth. One shop to another. And just as he was starting to regain control of his own limbs, a tangle of bunting flapped across his face. He tumbled over some hysterical chickens and started rolling down the road like a giant hairy butterball, clutching Dev tightly in his arms.

Dev's stomach lurched up and down, as the streets spun past his eyes.

CRUNCH! TINKLE! CRUMP!

'HYAAAAAAARRGHHH!' Boja squeezed Dev even tighter.

'HMMMFFFF!' Through a mouthful of red fur, Dev tried to agree.

There was one more loud *CRASH*, and then they came to a halt. Dev poked his head out to see where they were. A sweet, familiar smell caught his nose.

'Arnold's Waffle Shop!' he yelled, battling to tear off his cloak. 'Or at least what's left of it.'

Boja lay amongst the rubble, dazed. Then his nose twitched, his huge eyebrows rose up and his tongue smacked back into his mouth. 'WOH-FFLES!' he giggled, just as the walls either side of him collapsed, throwing shelf upon shelf of delicious waffles down into his wide-open mouth.

'No, no! Stop!' Dev tried to pull the waffles away from Boja's sticky fingers. 'You can't just take them!'

'Mine!' Boja shovelled more into his mouth. 'MINE!'

'Not yours,' Dev implored.

Boja thought for a minute, and then offered a clump of waffle between his finger and thumb.

'For me?' Dev smiled. 'Well, I guess that's something. At least you're sharing!'

As Dev reached out to take it, Boja slowly pulled the waffle away, until it was hovering around his own mouth.

'Boja . . .' Dev reached across Boja's belly, chasing the waffle. 'Boja, *share* it.'

Boja's bottom lip wobbled, his eyes wincing as if he was in pain. He glanced at the waffle, at Dev, back at the waffle, before slowly slipping it into his upturned mouth and chewing it so reluctantly it may as well have been a lump of mud.

'Mine,' Boja whimpered.

Dev folded his arms, one eyebrow raised at the

greedy robot bear. 'Right, well, there are clearly a few things you have to learn about manners,' he huffed.

Boja burped a little burp. It smelt sweet.

Dev slid from Boja's belly and heaved the big red bear up and out onto the street. He patted him down, picking dough and sprinkles out from his fur, tutting like a fussy parent.

Boja's attention, however, was elsewhere. He was staring at the bright orange sun just over the horizon, watching as it struggled to shine through a swirl of thick, grey clouds. He reached out an arm, tweaking his fingers as if he could reach it. As if he could pluck it from the sky and keep it for himself.

'Mine,' he repeated.

Dev pressed his shoulder into Boja's left buttock and, with all his might, began shoving him down one of the narrower alleys.

'Not yours,' he wheezed. 'None of this is yours.'

23
The Spindletree Forest

'Carry me!'

Dev could hear Mayor Bumblebuss's voice echoing high up into the sky. The crowd, too. They were angry. He knew they'd all be descending the mountain. They'd want to know what he'd done, and how he'd done it.

They'd want Boja.

So Dev led the big red bear to a place he thought they might be safe. Past his house, past the remains of his workshop and into the shadows of Spindletree Forest. Or at least what was left of it. The trees were bare; the ground a carpet of fallen spindletree needles. Every fern was withered, every flower dead.

Dev climbed onto a large rock, and crossed his legs.

'I must have missed something.' He tried to remember each and every page of the flember book. 'I thought I knew enough. I transferred the flember, and it worked, it *actually worked*.' He looked over to the bright, glowing bear. 'But it worked *too* well. You got *too much* flember. And now everything else is dying.'

Boja wasn't listening. He had found a solitary,

wilting danderfly poking out from a crack in the rocks, and as he reached out it blossomed between his fingers, its translucent leaves unfurling to reveal a perfect bubble of danderfly seeds inside. His face lit up with delight. His huge nose twitched towards the flower and he took a great big sniff of it. Such a sniff, in fact, the danderfly burst, and a bundle of danderfly seeds shot up his nostrils. He stumbled backwards, his right eye twitching, his left eye watering, his mouth stretching out like a gargoyle.

'AAAAAAA . . .' He winced. 'AAAAAAAA . . .'

The thought of Boja sneezing and giving away their location had Dev scurrying towards him. He jumped frantically around, pleading with Boja to stifle it, to hold it in, to just . . . keep . . . quiet.

'. . . *choo!*'

Boja was as stunned as Dev. Not for him a huge, booming splatterfest, but rather a delicate peep.

'. . . *Choo!*' He sneezed again. '*Choo! Choo! Choo!*'

With each sneeze, globules of flember snot flew from his nose. *Splat! Splat! Splat!* Onto the rocky ground. Against the thorny bark of the trees. *Splat! Choo! Splat!*

And then.

'CHOOOOOO!'

The most almighty sneeze ever sneezed. A thunderous roar that shook the ground beneath their feet. It blasted Boja into a spindletree, which swayed under his weight before it toppled and crashed into another. That, in turn, caught another, which caught another, and one by one a circle of spindletrees crashed loudly down around them in a plume of dust and splinters.

Dev stared at Boja, who stared right back, wide-eyed, with the expression you might expect of someone who had just accidentally flattened a section of forest.

'Well, at least it stopped you sneezing.' Dev wafted the dust away, to see not just a circle of stacked, fallen spindletrees, but moss upon them. Spots of grass beneath them. And flowers; beautiful, blossoming flowers, wherever Boja's snot had landed. He knelt to the ground, running his finger across a small patch of grass. It glowed in the low light of dawn.

'Maybe you got *all* of Eden's flember,' he gasped. 'I mean, every last drop. From every flower, and every pojoboplant, and every spindletree on the mountain.' He ran to Boja's side and stroked a finger across his fur. Flember trickled out. 'And maybe you can just . . . put it back.'

He leapt up, a huge smile across his face. 'When you sneezed, you sneezed out flember. See where it landed? The little flowers growing out from each patch?'

'It's . . . nice.' Boja beamed.

'Nice! Ha ha! Yes it IS! It IS nice! And we need more of it, Boja. A lot more of it. You need to do THAT, all over THIS!' He waved his arms frantically towards the rest of Spindletree Forest. 'You're just going to have to . . . *flemberise* everything!'

He grabbed Boja's paw, rubbing it down a spindle-tree trunk. It left a sparkling trail, which blossomed into beautiful green lichen.

Boja chuckled.

Taking Dev's lead, he went to a cluster of dried-out ferns, ruffling their dead stalks back into a full bustling plumage. He spun on his heels, firing his fingers – *Plink! Plink! Plink!* – pink and orange flowers spinning out wherever the flember landed. He butt-slammed the dusty earth, sending out ripples of thick grass. *Plink! Splat! Flump!* Wherever flember touched, beautiful, rich foliage returned, and this one little corner of Spindletree Forest looked more

231

beautiful than it ever had before.

Dev danced around in the middle of it all as if he were the conductor of an orchestra.

An orchestra of one.

His miraculous, magical friend.

'We can put it back,' Dev laughed. 'We can put all the flember back!' He stepped from the grass into the shadow of the other, dead spindletrees. 'We'll do it tree by tree, plant by plant. It'll take a while, but . . .'

He spotted a lone flemberbug on the ground. It appeared quite dead, its body a dull flaky brown, its legs folded in on themselves.

All but one.

'LIMPY!' Dev cried in horror. 'Not you too! Oh no, no, no, I'm so sorry!'

He turned to show Boja. 'Boja look, this is my friend. I hoped he might have escaped all this, but he didn't. You see? He's very unwell.

233

He needs some flember.'

'Flem-buhhh.' Boja gazed at the lifeless thing in Dev's hands.

'Just like the trees,' Dev said. 'He needs flember to live.'

Boja, as scared as he was fascinated, extended a large red finger to poke the insect. Wisps of flember swirled out, straining to find something to inhabit, sliding down Limpy's antennae and into his body. Then Limpy's legs began to twitch. His bum began to glow. Within moments he had righted himself, spread out his glittery wings and hopped up into the air. He bopped against Dev's nose, swayed one way, then the other, before fluttering back down into his open hands.

'Just like that!' Dev yelped. 'You did it, Boja, you brought him back to life!'

But Boja wasn't celebrating.

There was a change in him.

A panic in his eyes.

He gripped the newly revived spindletrees and, as he did, great washes of light trickled out from their bark, along the ground, snaking around Boja's feet before disappearing inside his fur. Sparkles floated across the air like pollen, surrounding him, sinking into him. All this flember, so bountifully thrown around just moments before, now returning to the big, terrified bear.

He backed himself against a stack of fallen trees, nervously patting down any stray wisps of flember before they could escape from his fur.

'It's *mine*,' he whimpered.

Dev knelt amongst the wilted ferns and the shrivelled flowers.

'Oh Boja, you need it too don't you.' He sighed. 'So how are we supposed to fix this now?'

24
The Savagery of Law

The wind whistled through the dead spindletrees, catching on the few remaining needles and playing a disjointed melody. It set Dev's teeth on edge. Limpy the flemberbug didn't appear to be enjoying it either, as he scuttled along Dev's arm, down his vest and hid inside his trouser pocket.

Then, there came a gnawing against Boja's buttock.

'Fervus?' Dev jumped to his feet.

'FEVV-US!' All the fear disappeared from Boja's face, as if he had completely forgotten the last few minutes.

Fervus, only just noticing the big red bear, leapt back in shock, then hunched down and growled through his teeth.

Boja giggled. 'Fevvus!'

Fervus edged back towards him, sniffing madly. Boja leant over and did the same, his sniffs so powerful they dragged the little goat off the ground and up into his left nostril.

'If you're here,' Dev said, pulling Fervus back out with a sound like the cork from a bottle. 'Then the rest of the village won't be far behind. And they'll have Mum with them, and Nonna.'

He passed Fervus to Boja and hopped back onto his rock. Limpy emerged too, fluttering up onto Dev's shoulder as if hoping for a better view.

Together they listened.

For anything.

But besides the deathly tune of the trees, not a single sound came.

'Hang on,' Dev whispered. 'Why aren't they looking for us?'

The walk out of Spindletree Forest wasn't easy. Since the nostril incident, Boja and Fervus had become firm friends, and it wasn't long before the bleating, the chuckling and the ground-shaking hops became too much for Dev to cope with.

'WOULD YOU BOTH,' he hissed, 'just be quiet. We're trying not to attract any attention.'

Fervus stood motionless as he stared into Dev's eyes. His cheeks puffed out. His quivering tail lifted up, and then . . .

Prrp!

A tiny fart, barely even a waft, but enough to send Boja into peals of laughter. Dev fussed around him, lifting his paws to his mouth, shoving him behind a tree. Anything to keep the big bear quiet.

And so it went on. Past the house. Fart. Giggle.

Across the broken bridge. Fart. Giggle. Back towards the marketplace. Fart. Giggle. Fart.

It was here that Dev finally spotted some other villagers – a number of anxious-looking Youth Guild cadets guarding the path into the Old Woods. So before they were seen, he bustled Boja and Fervus in the opposite direction. Down through the Middle Eden back streets, towards the Great Hall.

From where, finally, he could hear voices.

A whole lot of voices.

There were Guild out front, but Dev crept around the back, where the hall flattened itself against a steep wall of rock, and concealed the three of them in shadow. He sat Boja beneath the high window so that he could climb up his furry back, and then he

knelt down on top of his head.

'Keep still,' Dev whispered, pressing his face against the glass and peering inside.

Mayor Bumblebuss was yelling.

'ORDER! We'll not resolve ANYTHING unless we have order.' He checked the clock around his neck. 'Procedure must be followed. No time to waste. Tick, and indeed, tick.'

Surrounding him was a mass of villagers, their helmets all clonking together. They jostled and pushed against a barricade of Guild members. One broke through.

'My petunias are gone! My blue opals!' Agatha Bloom, from Agatha Bloom's Floral Adore-All, held up a rather pathetic display of withered flowers. 'What sort of flower shop doesn't have any flowers?'

'Never mind your flowers, what about our fields?' The farmers pushed out after her, throwing blackened corn stalks to the floor. 'The wheat, the corn. It's all dead. Not a drop of flember left in anything, not a DROP!'

The crowd started shouting over each other again.

'YOU DON'T NEED TO TELL ME,' the Mayor roared. 'It's barely morning, and already my Flember Day is RUINED. The Eden Tree, prize of our village, *dead*!'

Dev ducked down, as if it would save him from the memory of what he'd done, the people he'd hurt, the village he'd half-destroyed. But the guilt still stung.

Boja smiled up at him. As he did, however, one last danderfly seed must have dislodged inside his nostril, for his mouth stretched up and his eyes began to twitch and his whole head pulled back for another sneeze.

'NOPPPPPE!' Dev whispered, reaching down and pinching Boja's nostrils closed. Then, with his other hand, he gripped Boja's lips.

Boja's cheeks ballooned out.

'No sneezing,' Dev begged. 'Just hold it in. Please?'

Boja's eyes rolled back up towards Dev, and he nodded. Dev cautiously let go. He looked back through the window.

Percy had taken the floor. 'What Dev brought up to Shady Acres,' he said. 'It must be some kind of a machine. He said he *invented* it, didn't you hear? He invented a *machine*. A machine that took all of our *flember*.'

'It can't be true,' Bastor shouted above him. 'It just can't! You can't take flember out of the ground, it's impossible. It's *inconceivable*. How would he even do such a thing?'

The Mayor's fluffy white eyebrows creased down over his eyes. He shot a furious glance to Zerigauld, who was cowering beside his table.

'Something to do with a golden *heart*, apparently.'

'I'll not be blamed for any of this.' Zerigauld crawled out, his lip turning up to reveal his crooked teeth. 'That 'eart was my prize, my most beautiful acquisition! A sight for the soul! Had it for years I did, wouldn't dream of partin' with it.'

'Well now it beats inside a machine.' The Mayor beckoned to the Guild. 'And that machine is destroying our village.'

Only now could Dev see his mother, Ventillo and Santoro standing at the side of the crowd, flanked by Guild, kept away from the discussion. On the Mayor's command, however, Santoro was nudged out.

'Tell 'em it ain't so.' Zerigauld turned to Santoro, his beady little eyes shimmering. 'Tell 'em you didn't steal my 'eart, that you 'ad nothing to do with this mess. It's yer brother, int it. He done all this. Some ridiculous plan 'e done by himself.'

'You leave Santoro alone,' Ventillo shouted. 'You daft old bird. You miserable sausage!'

Zerigauld stiffened, flaring his nostrils. A nervous chatter started to build inside the Hall, which Mayor Bumblebuss swiftly silenced with a loud cough.

'Santoro,' the Mayor sighed. 'Were you involved? The theft? The . . . *machine*? Eden losing its flember? Were you involved in *any* part of this?'

Dev grimaced. Despite what Santoro had done and the resentment Dev felt, it was still painful to watch his brother being blamed for things which weren't entirely his fault.

'He's *innocent*!' Ventillo shouted.

'Santoro?' the Mayor repeated.

For quite some time, Santoro didn't reply. He stared back at the Mayor without even a flicker of emotion passing across his face.

Then his lips moved, but whatever he said was too quiet for Dev to hear.

'You're right. I *have* made my decision,' the Mayor snapped. 'Santoro, whatever you and your brother did, you have endangered our village, and we simply cannot stand for that. Guild, strip him of his colours.'

Guild members surrounded Santoro, gripping his tunic.

'You are no longer Youth Guild, you no longer have authority in this village,' the Mayor declared. 'And if you have any sense, you will stay *away* from your brother.'

They tried to remove his uniform but Santoro fought back, thrashing and writhing around until his clothes started to tear. Then someone pulled the Guild helmet from his head and his whole body

collapsed. Dev could see tears streaming down his cheeks.

And his own eyes began to glisten.

'—CHOOOOOO!' Boja suddenly boomed, lurching forwards and splattering Fervus with glowing blue snot.

'THEY'RE HERE!' the Mayor yelled, catching

Dev's eye through the window.

The Guild rushed the crowd, the crowd rushed the doors, and suddenly the whole village was clamouring for Dev and Boja.

25
Space Fleet

'This way!' a voice hissed. 'Lieutenant Dev, over here!'

It came from a crack in the rock face. Sam, still wearing a hedge, was crouched down inside.

'We can save you from that . . . that big red *space monster*!'

Dev slid down Boja's snotty arm and pulled him onto his feet. 'He's not a machine, he's not a monster. He's a *Boja*.'

'Well, whatever he is –' Sam squeezed back into the darkness, '– you might wanna follow me.'

Dev heard the doors of the Great Hall clatter open, and a sense of urgency rushed his veins. He dived after Sam, pulling Boja in between the narrow rock walls. It was no easy feat, but with Fervus on the outside nipping at Boja's buttocks, they managed to squeeze him through. Disappearing down, deeper, and deeper, and then out into the grey morning light of Lower Eden, beneath the arch of the main road, and along the brambles of The Wall. Down into Lower *Lower* Eden.

Home to the forgotten and the abandoned.

The perfect place to hide.

A few collapsed sheds gave way to a large overgrown field. There was grass beneath Dev's feet, trees rustling in the wind, moss and weeds covering everything like a blanket.

'Flember.' Dev breathed in the air. 'The village still has some left.'

'Commander Sam, you brought the monster *with you?*' Alice poked her head out from inside a barrel. 'You were supposed to be rescuing Lieutenant Dev *from* it!'

'He's not a monster!' Dev hurried Boja past them. 'He's a Boja. A *Boja*!'

'Boh-jah?' Reginald, still in his pig costume, peered out from a bunker made of old mattresses. 'He must be an undiscovered alien species!'

'Spee-scheez!' Arto popped up beside him.

'He's the only one of his kind,' Dev puffed. 'And I need somewhere to hide him!'

'Sir, yes, sir!' Reginald saluted. 'Prepare Space Fleet HQ for alien quarantine!'

Space Fleet HQ, otherwise known as Sam's tree-house, was an old, rickety shed, beneath which a rundletree had grown, and grown, eventually lifting it up between its twisting branches. Dev climbed

the rope ladder, crawled in through the doorway and cleared some space amongst the empty crisp packets. He then called for Boja, who found his own way in by climbing the tree, lifting off the entire roof and carefully wedging himself inside.

Once the roof was back on, Space Fleet HQ was virtually vacuum-sealed.

'We'll stand guard!' Sam declared, as he, Arto, Reginald and Alice assumed defensive positions around the foot of the tree. Each taking it in turns to be distracted by Fervus the goat.

'Thank you, Space Fleet,' Dev called down to them as he struggled to move around Boja's considerable bulk. 'We'll just hide here. At least until I can figure things out.'

'INTRUDER!' Reginald suddenly yelled, taking off his shoe and jabbing it towards the long grass. 'Who goes there?'

Mina cautiously stepped out. 'I . . . I followed Boja!'

'No girls allowed!' Reginald prodded the shoe into her belly.

'*I'm* a girl,' Arto shouted.

'Me too,' Alice added.

'Oh, sure, but no *other* girls. You're not, like, girls. You're . . . well, I mean you're *girls*. I mean . . .' Reginald's cheeks flushed red. 'Sorry. Yes. YOU MAY PASS. Sorry.'

'Mina, you shouldn't . . . *mmf* . . . have come.' Dev squeezed his head out through a window. 'Everyone in the village is looking for us.'

'He's so bright!' Mina gazed at Boja's beautiful blue glow. It shone out through the windows, out between the cracks in the treehouse walls. 'He's so pretty.'

Dev felt Boja's cheeks rise up in a smile.

'He was supposed to be a bigger version of your Boja Bear,' Dev said. 'He was supposed to keep *everyone* safe. But, well, things haven't quite worked out that way . . .'

Suddenly, Fervus bleated out an alarm and pointed his whole body back towards Middle Eden. Reginald took off his other shoe and stood behind him. The others grabbed what they could – bin lids, branches, Fervus – and together they reformed their defensive line in front of the tree.

'W-what's coming?' Sam asked.

'I'm not sure,' Dev whispered.

A light blinked out somewhere ahead of them. Then another. And another. Generators banged and popped. The mossy grass crinkled and turned brown as if a poison was flowing through it, and suddenly a huge crack ripped through the middle of it all. Down the rocky overhang, down into Lower Lower Eden, tearing across the field and straight up the middle of the rundletree.

'The land is dying!' Dev screamed, but it was too late. Space Fleet HQ collapsed into the split, dragging him and Boja down in a cloud of splinters and dust. Boja landed on his ample bottom, and Dev, in turn, landed on Boja. Limpy the flemberbug spun a few circles above them, before finally settling on Boja's nose.

'I'm OK!' Reginald shouted.

'Behhh!' Fervus agreed.

Silence.

And then some sniffles.

'Mina!' Dev cried, scrambling over the wreckage.

She sat beside the collapsed tree. Her eyes glistened, her lip quivered and she clutched her bandaged arm.

'It still hurts,' she said. 'It hurts *more*.'

Dev bundled her into his arms, and together they slumped onto the ground. The rest of Space Fleet surrounded them. Some tried to hug Mina. Others helplessly patted her from a distance. One apologised for poking her with a shoe. None of it helped. Her face erupted into a wobbling mess of tears.

'I need to fix this,' Dev whispered, trying to hold back his own. 'I need to fix all of this.'

Boja had been keeping himself occupied by watching Limpy pad back and forth across his nose. But his glance kept flicking over to Dev and Mina and, every time it did, his eyes would widen and his own lip would quiver. Eventually he hauled himself upright and cautiously crawled towards them. Mina recoiled out of instinct, but Boja reached out a big red paw and clasped it gently around her wrist. Wisps of flember spiralled out from his fur and around her whole arm, lighting it up so brightly Dev could see the shadow of the bones beneath her flesh. Mina's tear-stained cheeks flushed a warm red, and they rose into a beaming, wondrous smile.

'Sharing.' Boja smiled back.

'It doesn't hurt!' Mina waggled her fingers, before unravelling the bandage and waving her arm around.

'IT DOESN'T HURT AT ALL!'

She threw herself at Boja, burying her face into his belly. 'IFCH DUFSCHNT HUSCHT!' she repeated, gripping his fur and hugging him tighter than he knew what to do with. Then Space Fleet were upon them both, piling into the hug. And Fervus too, hopping across them like stepping stones, bleating in mad delight.

'Sharing.' Dev stood, staring in amazement at Mina's healed arm. 'He's sharing. He *understands*!'

Suddenly a cry went up from Middle Eden. There, on the overhang, Dev could see a crowd of villagers gesturing down.

'They've seen us,' Alice shouted. 'Boja's too bright to hide!'

Sam wrenched himself from the hug and jumped to attention. 'Lieutenant Dev, what are our orders?'

'I need to think,' Dev mumbled. 'I need to work this out. If Boja's ready to share a bit of his flember here, then he might be ready to share more of it with the village.'

Alice ran to what was left of Space Fleet HQ and started handing out bits of broken wood. 'Keep thinking! We'll defend you!' she cried. 'Space Fleet's last stand!'

'It'll take too long to run around, giving back the flember one tree at a time.' Dev paced back and forth. 'They'll capture him before he has the chance. They won't wait. They won't listen!'

Dev stared at the villagers. They had reached The Wall now, spilling down alongside it. Building in numbers, tumbling and swelling like a wave. Some splitting away to find their own paths, slipping and sliding down the hill, before being swallowed back into the mass.

It sparked a memory inside Dev's brain. The cold, damp cave. Ventillo. Watching the flember beneath them. *It rushes up inside the mountain,* she'd said.

'They're getting CLOSER!' Reginald called out.

Then it washes back down.

'Washes back down,' Dev whispered.

And suddenly, every thought he was having mashed together into one.

'*Gravity!*' he gasped. 'We can save the whole village in one go, if we can just get Boja back to the Eden Tree!'

26
Eden Cemetery

Although it was still only morning, thick rolling clouds had cast everything into a gloom. Lower Lower Eden, hidden beneath the overhanging rocks of the mountain, had now become almost as dark as night.

Bright, glowing Boja, however, undid all that. Dev tried to cover him with a Space Fleet flag, but it barely concealed his nose. Nope, he was like a shining lantern telling everyone where they were, so instead of creeping about in the dark, Dev decided, they'd just have to walk faster.

Space Fleet separated out. Sam, Alice and Fervus took the lead, since it was generally considered that they were the bravest. Reginald, Arto and Mina covered the rear. Limpy the flemberbug hopped between them, bringing forth giggles and snorts from whoever he landed on. Dev walked in the middle, alongside Boja, who grumbled and giggled from one second to the next.

'Are you sure this is the way to the Eden Tree?' Sam whispered, hanging back a little.

'It's . . . a different way.' Dev smiled.

'Oh no, no, no,' Reginald suddenly whined, clinging onto the ears of his pig costume. 'I know *exactly* where this path leads.'

'Stay on track!' Sam shouted.

'YOU stay on track,' Reginald snapped back. 'I should have

stayed at *home*! Don't you know where we're going?'

He pointed ahead, to where their path emerged from the shadows of Lower Lower Eden and wrapped itself around the mountainside. To where two tall iron gates hung from their hinges, squeaking gently back and forth in the breeze.

'KEM-EH-TREE.' Sam squinted. 'It's a kemetree?'

'CEMETERY! A GRAAAAAVEYARD!' Reginald hung on the As, to make it sound spookier.

The rest of Space Fleet,

including Fervus, shrieked.

'W-what's in a graveyard?' Mina cowered behind one of Boja legs.

'GHO-O-OSTS!' Reginald replied, pulling his pig ears down across his face.

'ARE THERE REALLY?' she yelped. 'Then I don't wanna go in!'

'You don't have to.' Dev smiled.

A shivering jumble of wide, terrified eyes stared back at him.

'We're supposed to be brave . . .' Sam mumbled.

Dev knelt down and clasped his clammy hand. 'You *are* brave. All of you. Mina and Fervus, you too. You've all helped me and Boja come this far.'

He held out a finger and Limpy fluttered down upon it. 'Here,' he said, tilting Limpy into Sam's hands. 'Lead Space Fleet home. Limpy will light the way.'

Sam saluted. 'Yes, sir! I can do that!'

The rest of Space Fleet saluted too. Reginald even nudged Mina to join in.

'You're honorary Space Fleet now,' he whispered.

She beamed with joy.

Dev saluted back. Boja tried to, but just poked himself in the eye. So, instead, he waved both his arms. And he kept waving while Dev pushed him on through the broken gates. Up the narrow path. Around the mountain. Even when the children had completely disappeared from view.

He just really enjoyed waving.

Their path was precarious. To the left was a steep drop down to the sea. A cold, stinging drizzle blew up and whipped against Dev's cheeks. To the right were trees – bare, twisted trees – their branches hanging down like long, deathly fingers. Their roots threading between hundreds and hundreds of tall, thin headstones, all stacked on top of each other.

Dev shivered and nuzzled deeper down inside his scarf. Between staring at the headstones and trying to keep Boja walking in a straight line, he almost didn't notice the figure sitting up ahead of them.

'I thought you might sneak this way,' Santoro called out.

'That's Dad,' Dev said. 'Don't sit on Dad.'

Santoro snorted, slid off the headstone and started walking towards his brother. His Guild uniform was torn, his helmet gone, but still he dragged his large sword along the ground behind him.

'I . . . I saw what happened in the Hall,' Dev stuttered. 'I know they threw you out of the Guild. And I'm sorry.'

Santoro bumped his shoulder against him. 'You've caused a lot of trouble today, Dev.'

'I can fix it,' Dev replied.

Santoro snorted. 'You know, if Dad was still here, he'd despair at what you've done to our village.'

'If Dad was still here,' Dev gritted his teeth. 'He'd want me to *fix* it.'

'No, he wouldn't. He'd ask why you can't just leave things alone.' Santoro leant in close to Dev's face. 'And then *he'd* fix it.'

Suddenly, Santoro swung his sword towards Boja. Dev instinctively leapt between them, slamming his hand onto his chest so his backpack ballooned out.

First from the back, pushing Boja away, then out front, throwing Santoro into the dirt. But within seconds Santoro was back on his feet and lunging towards them again.

'I'll carve our flember out of that machine!' he yelled.

Boja, his fur standing on end, his flember spinning out in great, wild arches, caught Santoro by the neck.

Tighter, he squeezed.

And tighter.

'Boja, let him go!' Dev jumped up at him. 'You can't do this. You can't *hurt* people!'

Boja looked down at Dev, and then opened his fist, dropping Santoro back onto the ground.

'No . . . friend,' he huffed.

'No, probably not,' Dev replied, still struggling to stuff his inflatable backpack down.

Santoro, a little redder of face and choking for air, leapt upon his brother instead. 'Your stupid experiments!' he roared, swinging his fists at Dev's head. One of his blows triggered Dev's helmet, and suddenly all its metal arms went off at once – lenses, lights, claws, grips, all folding out and tangling together into a mesh.

'I was trying—' Dev protested.

'I don't CARE what you were trying to do, Dev. I Do. Not. CARE.' With each word, Santoro wrenched away another metal arm. 'All I care about is this village. All I care about is us being safe. And at every turn, you're trying to undo that. Every new invention. Every single *thought you have*. Now our whole village is dying and it's your fault! You and your stupid machine!'

Boja growled and started towards them. Dev gestured to him to stay back.

'And even now, it's *me* picking up the pieces,' Santoro continued. 'Because that's what I do. I clean up your mess. It all falls on ME.'

Dev had always thought his brother was just mean. And now, suddenly, he saw something else in him too. Fear. It whistled through the cracks in his voice, glistened in the tears in his eyes. Santoro had been trying to keep his family safe, just as their dad would have done, but he didn't know how. No one had shown him.

And he was terrified of getting it wrong.

It nearly broke Dev's heart.

Santoro stopped. He slumped. He dropped the last of the metal claws and pushed himself onto his feet.

'Why do *I* have to step into Dad's shoes?' He

winced, walking over to his sword and dragging it up off the ground. He gripped both of his bruised, scratched hands around its handle and swung the blade back towards Boja.

'Why do *I* have to fix all your mistakes?'

27
What Was Left of Shady Acres

J ust then, something smacked Santoro across the face. It bounced across the path and came to rest beside Boja's foot.

It was a carrot.

Another whizzed past his head. A third he managed to bat away with his sword. But it was too late, the bait had been set. Fervus the goat was already charging full pelt towards him. Space Fleet followed, yelling and whooping. They threw more and more carrots towards Santoro, who tried to shield himself, but within seconds he had been toppled to the ground.

'We couldn't abandon you, Dev!' Sam yelled,

battering Santoro with one of Reginald's shoes. 'Not when you were being attacked by an *alien bounty hunter!*'

Fervus hopped back and forth, bleating wildly, inhaling carrots as if he'd never tasted one before.

'FEVVUSS!' Boja cheered.

Mina emerged from the scrum, taking hold of Boja's paw in one hand, Dev's in the other. 'RUN!' she shouted, pulling them both up the narrow shingle path.

Shouting arose behind them. Santoro had broken free of Space Fleet's attack and was racing after Boja, his sword still drawn. 'I'll save this village,' he roared. 'ME!'

Mina knelt down and rummaged through her backpack. First she pulled out Limpy, who tutted and clicked and then fluttered onto Dev's shoulder. Then, to Dev's surprise, she hauled out his old cheese canisters, and clipped them onto her heels, clicking them together. Something inside the canisters started to bubble, then billowed out in a great cloud of orange foam.

She looked to Dev with a glint in her eye.

'I been imbenting.' She grinned as the boots spun her round, then propelled her back down the hill. *BAM!* Helmet-first into Santoro's stomach. A cheer went up, Space Fleet bundled in, and they all disappeared inside the enormous plume of foam.

Boja poked out his tongue and licked droplets from his nose. He smiled, and went a little cross-eyed.

'Hibbicus beer.' Dev sniffed at the air. 'She was *right*!'

His heart swelled with pride.

'And she's bought us a few more minutes.'

Soon the cemetery was behind them, and the western peaks of Shady Acres rose into view. But this was not the Shady Acres Dev knew. Where bushy redfern trees had once grown, now only bare trunks stood. The grass had withered away, the soil had turned dusty and hard. Nothing swayed in the breeze, nothing hopped across the ponds.

No light shone.

Nothing breathed.

Dev's hand absent-mindedly gripped Boja's fur, as if trying to cling to something he hadn't broken yet. He sighed, a long, exhausted, sigh, as he stepped between the flemberbugs on the ground. Hundreds, if not thousands of them. Their legs curled into their bellies. A nervous Limpy scuttled down from Dev's shoulder, paused for a moment on his chest, then disappeared back inside his pocket.

Boja looked nervous too. He stood with his arms wrapped around himself.

'Mine,' he whispered.

Dev looked up at the Eden Tree. Its twisted branches, its withered trunk. Its roots, buckling up from the soil like the tendrils of a long dead monster.

'It's not all yours, Boja,' he sighed. 'You need to share . . .'

Suddenly Boja's nose started to twitch.

'WOH-FFLES.' He grinned, turning to see Arnold the waffle maker still sitting in the ruins of his half-destroyed waffle cart, his face as pale as if he'd seen a ghost.

'Oh no you don't,' shrieked Arnold.

But it was too late. Whatever thoughts Boja had been processing just moments before had all been thrown to the wind. Now all he could waffle was

waffledy-waffle. He powered towards Arnold. His belly rumbling. His tongue flapping out of his mouth.

'MINE!' he shouted before launching himself up into the air, and landing face-first in whatever was left of the Flember Day Special.

'I'm so sorry.' Dev helped Arnold to his feet. 'I didn't know you'd still be up here.'

'Ahhh, you've probably done me a favour.' Arnold shrugged, picking up a bobbleberry and delicately placed it on top of Boja's head. 'I got so obsessed with making this thing. SO obsessed. Forgot about everything around me. And for what? So this great lump could throw himself into it.'

Boja rolled onto his back, cramming great fistfuls of whipped cream into his mouth.

'Maybe we *both* got a little overambitious.' Arnold chuckled, putting his arm around Dev's shoulder. 'Difference is, though, I just made a big pile of waffles. You made something . . . *extraordinary.*'

Dev felt that sinking feeling in his stomach. The one he must have felt a million times, just today.

'It doesn't feel that way any more,' he replied. 'It feels like I've made a huge mess of everything.'

'I'll TELL you what you've made, lad.' The large, wobbling figure of Mayor Bumblebuss stormed through the wilted ferns. 'You've made a DANGEROUS MACHINE. And for that, you are hereby charged with *treason*.'

28
Persuasion

'Treason?' Dev cried.

'TREASON!' The Mayor lolloped towards him, waving his bejewelled hand at Boja. 'That *machine* sucked all the flember from our village, *you* built the machine, so *you* are guilty of treason.' His big, fluffy moustache barely concealed a smirk. 'And treason comes with the *heaviest* punishment. You're going outside The Wall.'

A handful of Guild members shuffled up behind him. At their helm was an uneasy-looking Bastor.

'Um, I'm sorry, sir,' he whispered into the Mayor's ear. 'But a charge like treason requires intent. You would have to *prove* that Dev intended to cause all this.'

Mayor Bumblebuss arched an eyebrow and clicked his fingers. Like a well-trained rat, Zerigauld Sourface scurried out between the Guild's legs.

'Oh, but intent we do *'ave*.' Zerigauld unfurled Dev's bedsheet.

'If you had been doing your duty, Bastor,' the Mayor sniffed, 'you would have gone, like Sourface did, to the remains of Dev's workshop. And there you would have gathered evidence. Evidence like this – a clear indication of what Dev planned to do, and how he planned to do it. A precise blueprint of his *flember extraction machine.*'

'Boja was only ever designed to take a bit of flember. A spoonful!' Dev protested.

'Meh, meh, meh.' Zerigauld hobbled towards him. 'What 'urts me, boy, what cruelly stains my *own* good nature, is that you used my 'EART to DO such a TERRIBLE thing!'

He stuck a claw-like finger into the sheet, right where Dev had drawn the golden heart inside Boja's chest.

'DIDN'T YOUS?'

Dev silently nodded.

'A confession!'

'So, that's theft –' the Mayor counted on his pudgy fingers '– on top of irresponsible robot building, disrupting Flember Day, fleeing arrest, smashing through half of Eden, oh and, of course, *TREASON!*'

'We'll be chuckin' you over The Wall!' Zerigauld cackled. 'Out into the Wildening!'

The Mayor checked his clock. 'And since time is of the essence, we'll skip the formalities. Dev P. Everdew, you're obviously guilty. Do you have any last requests before we escort you out of the village?'

'Yes! I just need a few more minutes with Boja!'

Before the Mayor could even say a word, Dev had grabbed Boja's paw and hauled him onto his feet.

'Boja, you need to come with me. We need to *show* them what you've learnt.'

Boja followed, but his attention was elsewhere. His fur was matted thick with waffles and cream, and nothing was going to distract him from this glorious turn of events. Whatever Dev was saying, Boja was far too busy to listen, as he plucked off great waffley wedges, popped them into his mouth, and chewed *very* contentedly.

It worked in Dev's favour. Boja didn't notice the dead flemberbugs, or even realize where he was being led, until they reached a hollow in the roots of the

Eden Tree. Only then did he catch sight of the huge dead tree looming over them both.

And a clump of hairy waffle fell from his mouth.

'Remember what you did in the Spindletree Forest?' Dev said. 'When you brought everything back to life. All the lights? All the colours? How magical it all looked?'

Boja kept staring up at the tree.

'Do you think you can do that again, but from up here? Release your flember through this tree, so it all flows back down into the village?'

'STOP THAT! WHAT ARE YOU TELLING THE MACHINE?' the Mayor shouted, striding up towards them.

Still staring at the tree, Boja's eyebrows sank into a deep frown. 'Not a machine,' he huffed.

'And do you remember when we were at the treehouse, with Mina?' Dev spoke quicker now.

A smile pinched into Boja's cheeks.

'How happy she was when you shared some of your

flember with her? Well, think how happy you'll make the *whole village*, just by sharing a bit more.'

He tugged on Boja's finger.

'It's all down to you, Boja.' Dev smiled. 'Only *you* can save our village.'

Tears began to wobble in Boja's eyes. 'Scared,' he mumbled.

'I know.' Dev winced. 'You shouldn't have to do this. I'm so, so sorry, Boja.'

'I'm not.' Santoro barged past the Mayor. His sword was as long as he was, and nearly as wide, yet he swung it as if it weighed nothing.

'Out of my way, Dev,' he growled. 'I'm going to carve up your machine.'

29
A Good Heart

'That's the stuff!' Mayor Bumblebuss cheered. 'Get our flember out of that thing and you're back in the Guild, lad! With honours!'

Other villagers had started to appear. Some from the mob who had followed Boja through the cemetery, and others from the village, who had seen his bright flember glow from a distance. And yet, no one in the crowd appeared to share the Mayor's revelry.

They were quiet.

They were curious.

'He'll give his flember back.' Dev spread himself in front of Boja. 'He will!'

'I'd rather just take it,' Santoro snarled.

'Get away from him!' Commander Sam shouted, sliding down into the dirt beside them. Reginald followed, then Arto, Alice, Mina and Fervus. They formed a line in front of Boja.

'Boja's our friend!' Reginald punched at the air with both his shoes on his hands. 'And Space Fleet stand by their friends!'

'SPACE FEET!' Arto cheered.

Santoro rolled his eyes. 'You do realise you're all so short that I can just aim above you, right?'

He didn't have the chance to try. With a click of the Mayor's fingers the Guild descended upon the Space Fleet cadets, lifting each of them up off the ground. Then they turned on Dev, wrenching him from around Boja's waist. Dev screamed, which brought forth from Boja a huge, ground-shaking roar. But the rest of the Guild held firm, their swords outstretched, the bright, blazing bear unable to get past them.

And then, in an instant, all Boja's fury was gone.

Panic gripped him instead, and he turned, clambered onto the thick roots of the Eden Tree, then shuffled up its trunk. Higher and higher he went, to the very top, to the thinnest branches that would take his weight.

Where he then clung on for his very life.

The Mayor made a noise not unlike a chicken being kicked. 'IT . . . IT RAN AWAY!'

'He's SCARED!' Dev cried out from the tussle.

'He SHOULD be.' Santoro embedded his sword into the side of the tree with an almighty *THUNK*! Then he hauled it back out and *THUNKED* it back in again. 'GET DOWN!' he yelled. 'GET DOWN, GET DOWN!'

Dev thrashed around, trying to break free from the Guild but they wouldn't let go. All he could do was stare at the brightly lit bear hiding way, way up in a tree.

Swaying from side to side.

Staring back at him in absolute terror.

Dev slumped to his knees. His mind was racing, trying to think of something, anything to undo this mess. But there was nothing. All his brilliant ideas and now, when he needed one the most, there was *nothing*.

Santoro had been right.

Their dad would have been so disappointed in him.

'It's over, Dev,' his mother whispered, kneeling beside him and slipping her arms around his waist.

'You've done so well. You've tried *so* hard. But the flember was never Boja's in the first place. It belongs to the village.'

She pressed her cheek against his.

'We need it to *live*.'

Something inside Dev started to crumble. And as it did, it took other parts of him with it, until all of his insides tumbled deep, deep down into the lowest reaches of his soul. He let out an exasperated gasp, tears streaming from his eyes. His mother pulled him in, burying his face into her shoulder.

'I can't save him,' Dev sobbed, his whole body shaking uncontrollably for what may have only been moments, but seemed like forever. Eventually he lifted his head up and looked at the Eden Tree, up towards the big, red, amazing bear at the top of it.

The big, red, amazing bear who was still staring right back at him.

No panic in his eyes any more. No fear.

Just a kindness.

'I'm sorry,' Dev winced.

Boja nodded his head, said something Dev couldn't hear, and then gripped onto the tree a little tighter.

And a great flash of light consumed Shady Acres.

DOOMPF! it went.

And another.

DOOMPF!

Huge, blinding bursts of flember, pulsating out from Boja's fur.

DOOMPF!

DOOMPF!

DOOMPF!

'That sounds –' Dev wiped at his eyes. '– like his *heart*.'

And then.

The Eden Tree lit up like a thunderbolt. Its branches curled out, bustling with sparkling white leaves. Its roots shimmered like long, winding rivers. In waves it came, with each deafening *DOOMPF* of Boja's heart. Grass sprang up beneath the crowd's feet. Bilderflowers, pojoboplants, towering redferns, each growing bigger and brighter than before. It spilled from Shady Acres like a flood, flushing through the trees, twisting the corn stalks back into shape, glittering across the surface of the rice paddies. Emerald green moss rolled through the Old Woods like a carpet. Water bubbled up into the streams. Down into Middle Eden, ivy crawled across the houses. The generators spluttered back into life. All the lantern strings flickered above the streets, each of them now burning a bright, beautiful blue.

The clouds above Shady Acres broke and sunlight – warm, rich sunlight – shone down upon the cheering crowd. It lit up the

flemberbugs, the flipping, flop-
ping flemberbugs. Their bodies
glowed. Their legs clicked. And then
one by one they were up, and they were away.
CLIK-CLIK-CLIK, in one glorious wave above
the trees and rooftops of Eden.

Over The Wall.

And then somewhere far, far away, where they
belonged.

But Dev barely noticed any of it. He had been
watching Boja the whole time. He had been listening to the *DOOMPFS* as they became fainter, and
fainter. With each one, Boja had slid a little further
down the tree. Still he clung on to the trunk, but
the branches flipped him one way, then the other,
until finally his huge, saggy body slid all the way
back down to the roots.

His once blazing flember now barely a glow.

With one almighty push, Dev broke
free of the Guild, ran across Shady

Acres and threw himself into Boja's red fur. Listening for whatever heartbeat he could find.

But it was just a whisper.

Boja was dying.

30
You Can't Save Everything

'OK that's enough.' Dev tried to pull Boja's arm away from the tree. 'Boja, stop now. You've given enough back.'

'ALL OF IT!' the Mayor roared. 'Every last drop of the stuff, back where it belongs!'

'But he's DYING!'

The Mayor snorted. 'Not fast enough.'

'Boja, get away from the tree,' Dev pleaded. 'Let GO of it!'

He stopped pulling and instead he pushed. Leaning his whole weight in, yelling, screaming, channelling every last ounce of energy. But a big heavy bear weighs as much as a big heavy bear, and

Boja wouldn't move from the tree.

'LET GO!' Dev screamed through a mouthful of fur.

Boja looked down at him, and slowly, ever so slowly, a wide, goofy smile spread across his face.

'Shhh-aring,' he slurred.

'But you're dying,' Dev sobbed. 'You're DYING!'

Whatever Boja said in reply, it disappeared into a whisper. His eyes closed, and his breathing slowed, and to Dev's horror the last few wisps of Boja's flember started to slip away.

And then something else slammed into him. Santoro. His arms buried into Boja's side, his heels dug into the ground, his whole body leaning in for the push.

'Dad would want me to help,' Santoro growled, and with a renewed strength Dev piled in too, both of them wrenching Boja away and tumbling his massive body onto the ground. The tree plunged back into darkness – bare, withered darkness, its leaves fading from the branches as if they'd been ghosts.

An incredible cracking sound
filled the sky and its mighty trunk
split right down the middle,
curling it into two halves of the
same, dead tree.

Everyone held their breath,
praying that Shady Acres wouldn't
turn again too. It didn't. The
grass remained green, the flowers
bloomed, and all that grew
around the remains of the Eden
Tree still hummed with just the
right amount of flember.

A few villagers audibly sighed with relief.

'MY TREE!' Mayor Bumblebuss finally shrieked.
He turned towards Boja, his red face wobbling with
anger. 'Guild! Seize that machine! IT STILL HAS
THE TREE'S FLEMBER!'

The Guild shuffled nervously.

'WHAT ARE YOU WAITING FOR? Confound
you, I'll do it MYSELF!' The Mayor grabbed a sword

and charged towards Boja. But Santoro was ahead of him, swinging his own sword just short of the Mayor's nose.

'You could have been a hero,' the Mayor growled, running his blade against Santoro's. 'All you had to do was take apart that machine.'

'His *name* is Boja.' Bastor stepped alongside Santoro, his sword drawn and pointed towards the Mayor. 'And he's not a machine.'

'Of course it is!' the Mayor shrieked in such a high pitch it was barely audible. 'You saw the plans. Guts full of metal. Like a MACHINE!'

Bastor didn't flinch. 'He was going to sacrifice himself for our village. He made that choice. No *machine* would do such a thing.'

Others from the Guild followed Bastor's lead,

303

their swords drawn with his. And then the villagers,
too, gathered alongside. Percy kept his distance, and
Zerigauld started crawling away, but aside from them
every adult, every child, and a goat, circled around
the Mayor.

'That bear is *alive*,' Arnold piped up.

'A living creature,' Rosa added. 'Just like the rest
of us.'

'BUT . . . *Fnnpp* . . . *RRFFFF*!' the Mayor spat
and burbled. 'This is DISSENT! I'll throw you ALL
outside The Wall!'

Bastor removed his Guild helmet. 'Mayor Simpius P. Bumblebuss, I . . . I believe you to be acting against the will of the people,' he said. 'And so, by section . . . section . . .'

'Twenty-three,' Amy whispered.

'Section twenty-three of the Eden constitution, I request three more Guild votes to have you removed from your post.'

Without a second's hesitation, every hand in the Guild rose into the air. And behind them, every villager's too. Bumblebuss's mouth fell open, setting

off a chain reaction across his seven chins.

He turned back to Santoro. 'And you,' he snarled. 'You double-crossing coward. Your father would be *ashamed!*'

Santoro stared intently back. 'Nah.' He smiled. 'I think he'd be proud.'

'I SHOULD HAVE THROWN YOUR WHOLE FAMILY OUT—' The Mayor was cut short by a slap across the cheek.

Amy Everdew stood beside him, her face a dark crimson, her teeth gritted. Her body heaving with rage.

'You STOP talking about my family,' she said.

Bastor carefully unstrapped the Mayor's helmet,

wiped the sweat from inside and then put it on in place of his own.

'Mayor Bumblebuss, thank you for your service, but I shall stand in until the Guild votes for a new Mayor of Eden.'

Upon his nod, two Guild members stood alongside Bumblebuss, lowered his sword and politely gripped his arms. Bumblebuss, now looking less like a mayor and more like a sad old man in a fancy dressing gown, stared around in shock.

Dev, however, was far more concerned with Boja, the huge, immovable lump lying face down in the grass. He couldn't hear a heartbeat, couldn't even feel Boja breathing.

There was nothing.

He gently shook the bear back and forth, trying to get a response. 'Please,' he sobbed. 'Boja please.'

The crowd fell silent.

Even the breeze seemed to stop.

Then, suddenly, Boja's whole body lurched forwards with a HICCUP. He rolled onto his back, exhausted, half asleep, staring into the sky.

HICCUP!

'You're OK!' Dev screamed, flinging himself into Boja's belly, revelling in the gentle *DOOMPF DOOMPF DOOMPF* of his heart. His fur was fluffy, his eyes were glinting, his tummy was rumbling and his flember had calmed right, right down.

'I SHARED!' Boja chuckled.

Then Space Fleet were upon them, and together they rolled around in the lush, dewy grass, laughing and screeching and hiccupping with joy.

'Not yet!' A shape came bustling through Shady Acres. A short, wide shape, which clattered and jangled as it walked. A glowing banana bobbing out

in front of it. 'No celebrating yet. If that tree is to
die, then it needs Jikanda.'

Ventillo stopped for a moment to catch her breath.
Then she stared incredulously at the rest of the crowd.

'What are you all waiting for?' She clapped her
hands, as if herding pigs. 'Jikanda. JIKANDA!'

31
Jikanda

The crowd made their way towards the Eden Tree and all held hands around it. Dev, his mother and Boja squeezed in. Dev held one of Boja's paws, Ventillo the other. Further along he saw Santoro, and then Arnold, Bastor and Rosa. Percy too, who glowered back and made a show of grabbing Mina's hand. Then he paused, realised which hand he'd taken, and marvelled at how it had miraculously healed.

Only ex-Mayor Simpius Bumblebuss refused to join in. He sat to one side, helmet-less, leaning back on his ample bottom, arms folded across his chest.

'You can't do this,' he huffed.

'Join us. Please.' Bastor beckoned.

'You can't just let that tree stay dead,' Bumblebuss insisted. 'Cut up the machine, take its flember out, put it back where it belongs. Be quick about it.'

Dev squeezed Boja's paw a little tighter.

'Flember flows between us *all*,' Ventillo shouted back. 'It gets *shared*. You know that as well as anyone, Bumblebuss. None of us wanted to lose the Eden Tree, but right now it's the bear's turn to hold its flember.'

The Mayor harrumphed loudly.

'The best *we* can do is thank the tree for a life well lived.' She smiled reassuringly towards Dev. 'So that's what we're going to do.'

'Right, well . . . let me try and remember how the prayer goes.' Bastor tried to cough over his nerves.

'Treacherous,' Bumblebuss grumbled.

'Villagers,' Bastor shouted over him. 'We've all had a difficult Flember Day.'

The crowd murmured.

'In offering flember to one, we had to lose it from another.' Bastor lowered his head in prayer. 'And so,

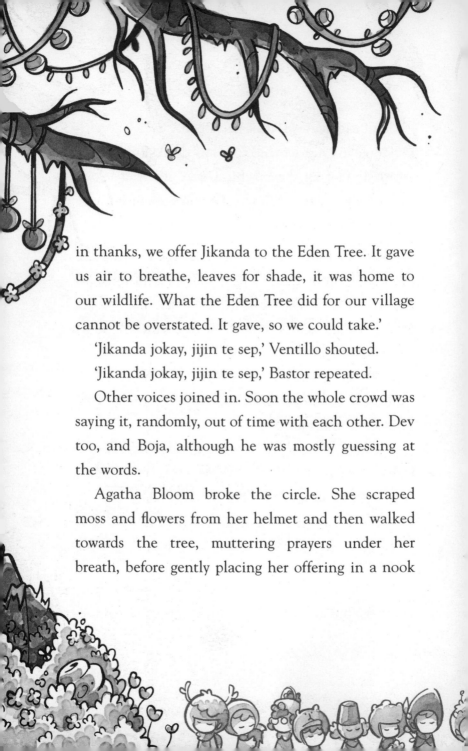

in thanks, we offer Jikanda to the Eden Tree. It gave us air to breathe, leaves for shade, it was home to our wildlife. What the Eden Tree did for our village cannot be overstated. It gave, so we could take.'

'Jikanda jokay, jijin te sep,' Ventillo shouted.

'Jikanda jokay, jijin te sep,' Bastor repeated.

Other voices joined in. Soon the whole crowd was saying it, randomly, out of time with each other. Dev too, and Boja, although he was mostly guessing at the words.

Agatha Bloom broke the circle. She scraped moss and flowers from her helmet and then walked towards the tree, muttering prayers under her breath, before gently placing her offering in a nook

of the tree's roots. Others followed, each taking the decoration from their helmet and presenting it to the tree. They tucked mushrooms inside its hollows. Smeared mud across its bark. Hung vines from its withered branches.

Whispering their own little prayers as they did.

'I . . . I don't have anything to offer,' Dev whispered to his mother.

'I think you do.' Amy smiled, nodding towards Dev's shoulder. For there sat Limpy the flemberbug, fluttering his wings and blinking in the daylight.

'Limpy!' Dev grinned. 'You stayed with us!'

Limpy waddled out onto Dev's hand, glowing

gently with flember. He rubbed his good legs together – *CLIK CLIK CLIK* – before taking off, drifting wonkily past Dev and Boja, over the crowd and towards the remains of the Eden Tree. There he landed, in amongst the moss and the ferns, the flowers and the mud, busily nudging his surroundings into the shape of a nest.

'A new colony, perhaps.' Ventillo clasped her hands together in delight. 'Right here in Eden! Oh wouldn't that be something.'

Ex-Mayor Bumblebuss, who, aside from a few snorts and scoffs, had been quiet during the ceremony, allowed his loudest snort of all.

'See? *THIS* is how flember works!' Ventillo glared at Bumblebuss. 'It finds new life.'

She smiled up at Boja.

'It found Boja. And he deserves flember just as much as everyone else.'

'Bojaaaaa!' Mina yelled, breaking from the circle and piling into Boja's legs.

Boja giggled, and then Space Fleet were upon him too. Clambering around him. Chanting his name. Other villagers edged forwards. They stared up in amazement. Poked Boja. Stroked him. And then, when they felt comfortable enough, absolutely buried him in questions.

'Boja,' Acting Mayor Bastor interrupted as he squeezed to the front of the crowd. 'Look after your flember. You have a duty, now, to carry it well.'

Boja nodded, then suddenly looked very panicked. As a hush fell upon the crowd, a gentle gurgle rose up through his throat and, before he could catch it in his paws, a delicate burp had slipped out of his mouth.

The crowd OOH-ed with delight.

'Welcome to Eden,' Bastor laughed.

A riotous cheer went up. Helmets were flung into

the air. Space Fleet went wild, running huge circles around the crowd, closely followed by a bewildered, bleating goat.

Dev felt his mum's hand slip into his.

'Boja's your responsibility now.' She smiled. 'It's about time you had some of that.'

32
The Fix

The crowd made its way down from Shady Acres, through the Old Woods. Everything was green again, everything *alive*. Birds sang. Leaves rustled in the breeze. Villagers plucked at the flowers as if they'd never seen such things before. This was quite a different procession from the one that had climbed up here this morning, but it was just as excited. A boy and his huge red bear, followed by a crowd of people. People who only wanted to touch Boja. To stare, wildly, at Boja. To marvel at how this creature could even exist at all.

'There's time for all that later,' Acting Mayor Bastor huffed, swatting their poking fingers away from Boja's belly. 'The marketplace is a mess of smashed tents. There are huge rips across the street. A lot of things need rebuilding, not least Arnold's Waffle Shop.'

Arnold's face went very, very grey indeed. 'What? What happened to my waffle shop?'

'The point is, we've a village to fix. And Dev, if you made Boja for the reasons you said you did, we'd greatly benefit from his help.'

Boja raised his arms in the air, a great cheer across his face.

'I think that means he'd love to,' Dev laughed.

'WAFFLES!' Boja shouted over him. 'WAFFLES, WAFFLES, WAFFLES!'

He turned, ploughed through the crowd and scooped Arnold up into a huge, crushing embrace. 'WOH-FFLES,' he boomed again, kissing the confused-looking waffle maker on the cheek.

'W-what did you do to my shop?' Arnold winced.

Boja pushed his way back to the front of the crowd, clutching Arnold like a grumpy dolly.

'WAFFLES!'

The marketplace was a bigger mess than Dev had remembered. All the destroyed stalls. The torn flags. Zerigauld's antique shop, still missing a big chunk of its wall. A line of shops Boja had bounced off or rolled through. All the buildings hit by his head, his belly, or his bottom. And all those gaping cracks in the ground, tearing up the street like huge claw marks.

There was a lot to do.

A lot to *fix*.

Dev smiled. Cleared his throat. Readjusted his helmet.

'Right –' he turned to Boja '– let's get started.'

'We'll help!' Sam and the rest of Space Fleet ran out around them. They each scooped up a small pile of debris – wood, soil, cold cuts of meat – and threw them into Boja's arms. Soon, Boja was carrying huge mounds away from the marketplace, and coming

back, arms empty, ready for the next. After four or five loads, however, Dev realised he was just dumping it all around the back of Zerigauld's shop, so it took a little more time to dispose of it properly. But he could see how much Boja was enjoying himself. This huge bear could lift whole trees. Lean buildings back into place. Fill the cracks in the street with rubble, before patting them down with wet mud. With Boja's help, every job was getting done ten times faster.

The Guild got stuck in too. Using their skills, their trades, to patch and rebuild. Every villager helped where they could, from the youngest to the oldest – carrying, hoisting, hammering and planting, whatever they could do to repair the village. The only exception was Zerigauld, hiding in the gloom of his shop, sneering at anyone who passed by his window. And Simpius Bumblebuss, whose sulk was so deep and so damp he refused to even lift a finger.

For everyone else in Eden, however, this was an event to *enjoy*.

It was evening by the time a small crowd had amassed outside Arnold's Waffle Shop. And yet, despite Boja's chants of, 'WAFFLES, WAFFLES, WAFFLES,' there were no waffles here. Nor was there a roof, or all that many walls. Just Arnold, sitting on a big pile of rubble.

'It's all gone,' he sobbed. 'My machinery's broken. My home is in pieces.'

'Dev can fix it,' someone in the crowd shouted.

'Yeah, go on, Dev. Come up with something!'

As more and more villagers cheered him on, Dev felt a swell in his chest, a burst of pride through his veins, and an excitable grin spreading across his face.

'Right!' He clonked the side of his helmet. 'Let's get thinki—'

His helmet ground and clanked, but no thinking bulb came out. He tugged on the straps, but no arms appeared, no lenses, no clamps. Just metal stubs and a shower of sparks.

'Oh, yeah,' Dev grumbled. 'No matter, I'll work without it!'

He paced back and forth, staring furiously at the ground. Occasionally he would stop and exclaim 'A-HA!' before dismissing the idea with a waft of the hand. Then he'd do another lap in front of the rubble, mumbling to himself.

Finally, to the great relief of his audience, he came upon a solution.

INVENTION 502: The Waffle Transportation Network

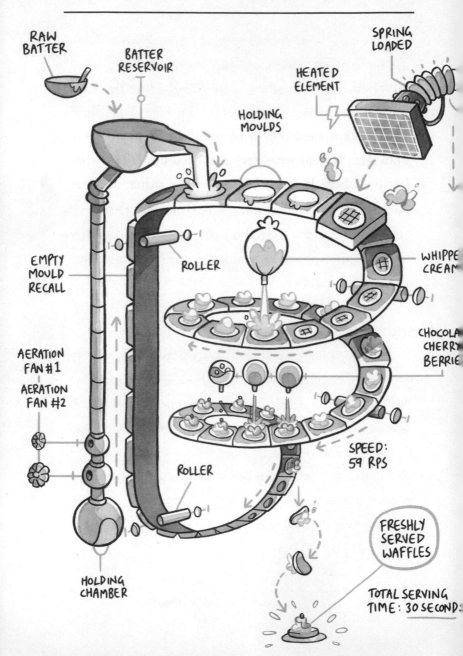

RAW BATTER

BATTER RESERVOIR

HEATED ELEMENT

SPRING LOADED

HOLDING MOULDS

EMPTY MOULD RECALL

ROLLER

WHIPPED CREAM

CHOCOLATE CHERRY BERRIES

AERATION FAN #1

AERATION FAN #2

ROLLER

SPEED: 59 RPS

HOLDING CHAMBER

FRESHLY SERVED WAFFLES

TOTAL SERVING TIME: 30 SECONDS

While Dev set to work building his device, Boja, Space Fleet and the rest of the crowd were all tasked with clearing the rubble. Needless to say, Boja did most of the heavy lifting, but, under Percy's watchful eye, Mina turned out to be quite an impressive site manager. She sat with Fervus tucked under one arm, her own Boja Bear tucked under the other, and her legs dangling over the edge of next door's balcony, as she barked instructions to every Space Fleet cadet, Guild member and villager regardless. With everyone working together, they managed to not only rebuild Arnold's Waffle Shop, but *improve* it.

Sort of.

Still it had no roof, and the walls were just piles of broken stone. Call it . . . rustic. Smaller rocks and debris were stacked into piles to serve as chairs or tables or, where they didn't look anything like chairs or tables, they could be sculptures. That was up to the customer. Not only that, but the shop now had a water feature in the middle. All agreed that it was a great talking point, and any mention of it being a burst water pipe would be unfair to an otherwise happy accident.

'It looks lovely.' Percy sat beside Mina, tenderly holding her hand. 'My little girl did well.'

'Done!' Dev triumphantly cried, standing back to admire his Waffle Transportation Network. It stood tall amongst the wreckage, a fairground ride of poles, gears and conveyer belts, all perched atop a wobbly mess of scaffolding.

'It's beautiful!' Arnold cheered. 'Does it work?'

'There's only one way to find out!' Dev turned the largest handle. 'Start making waffles!'

Arnold mixed up a large bowl of sugary batter, clambered to the top of the contraption, and dropped a great dollop into the batter reservoir. 'Boja, would you be my first customer?' he asked, and within what seemed like a fraction of a second Boja was sitting at the other end of it all. His drooling mouth open wide below the conveyor belt.

The waffles were toasted, slathered with cream, and decorated with toppings, all while sl-o-w-ly trundling towards Boja. The first one plopped onto his tongue. He shrieked with glee, chewing it over and over, savouring it with each and every taste bud. Then the next one came. And the next. And soon a steady line of hot, sugary waffles were tumbling down into Boja's mouth.

Boja was enraptured. Ecstatic. His eyes closed and he chomped. And chomped. Then he flung out his arms and hugged Dev so tightly it felt like one of them might burst. When he finally pulled away, they were both crying. Dev, because he hadn't been able to breathe, and Boja because he was just so flipping happy about waffles.

33
An Everdew Family Meal

News of Arnold's new waffle shop spread fast, and soon a larger crowd huddled in the streets around it. They basked in the shop's sweet, sugary warmth and chomped down on every new waffley combination Arnold could come up with. His wife, Nomilie, let their children join in the feast, while she affectionately wrapped her arms around Arnold's neck.

'Nice to have you back,' she hummed in his ear.

For most, that's how Flember Day ended – with a profound sense of thankfulness. The village had its flember back. And a new villager too. A huge, furry, miraculous villager. One who was currently handing out hot waffles, proudly yelling, 'I'M SHARING!' at everybody who took one.

As the pink skies of evening became the twinkling blacks of night, the crowd slowly filtered away. Space Fleet's numbers dwindled as their parents carried them home (after they had each hugged Boja goodbye). Mina gave Boja the biggest hug of all, then one for Dev too. Finally, amongst cheers from the stragglers, Acting Mayor Bastor arrived. He was wearing his new mayoral robes over his Guild uni-form and, to be honest, they didn't fit so well. A little tight around the shoulders. Enough to make him look uncomfortable, as he tugged at the fluffy trim and tried to keep the hem off the ground.

'Goodnight, everyone.' He nodded, scooping a sleeping Fervus up in his arms. 'Maybe tomorrow will be quieter, eh?'

The few remaining villagers waved him goodbye, and then they too wandered away, leaving only Arnold, his family and Dev. And, of course, Boja, who was leaning against the houses opposite, his body half-asleep but his mind, now filled with waffle sugar, apparently racing. He giggled. He twitched. He kept trying to catch the fireflies buzzing around his head. Eventually, it all became too much, and with one large belch he rolled forwards onto his face. And there he lay, gently snoring into the cobblestones.

'Time to take him home.' Santoro stepped out from one of the alleys. He had changed from his torn, dirty Guild uniform, and was now wearing just a smock, trousers and no helmet at all.

Dev was struck by how relaxed he looked.

'Thank you,' Dev said, as they grabbed a large red arm each, and started dragging the relentlessly heavy bear back home. 'For what you did up in Shady Acres. For helping to save Boja.'

'I thought he'd be more use to the village than a big old tree,' Santoro admitted. 'Aaaand it was sort of my fault you got in this mess in the first place.'

'You mean the heart?'

'I shouldn't have done that.'

They pulled Boja on in silence. Down the dusty

little path. Over the crumbling stone bridge. Up towards the front of the house.

'I'm glad you did,' Dev finally said, catching sight of a smile as it glimmered across Santoro's face.

The front door flew open, and their mother leapt out to meet them. 'You're back!' she exclaimed, helping the brothers to squash Boja in through the front door. Once inside, he crushed an armchair, fell over another, put his foot through a sofa and clonked his head against everything he could conceivably clonk his head against.

But Amy wasn't upset. Quite the contrary. She stared at Boja with amazement in her eyes. 'I still can't believe you . . . *built* him,' she gasped, while Santoro helped her hang the door back on its hinges.

Dev stood for a moment, soaking in the atmosphere. The house was warm. Lanterns flickered on the walls. The pipes above them gently *DINK-DINK-DINKED* with the sound of bees. Boja, fascinated, and a little more awake, started *DINK-DINK-DINKING* back.

'What we all need is a family *dinner*.' Ventillo barged the front door back open with a large wooden crate. 'Fire up the stove! I brought my best parsnips.'

'It's already going.' Amy gestured to a large pan of bubbling water. Speckled green eggs bobbed up and down in it. 'Mum, you brought apples.'

'Parsnips,' Ventillo replied, peering closely at her crate full of bright green apples. 'Oh, bother. Well it's not my fault, my banana's running out. I can't see properly.'

She pulled the banana from her helmet and handed it to Dev. Then she pulled a potato out from her pocket and slapped her hand against it. The banana flickered a couple of times, before its light faded out completely.

'Looks like I'm staying here tonight,' she said, grabbing plates from the cupboard. 'Duck eggs and apples for dinner. It'll be fine. Long as we're all here, we'll see Flember Day out, as a family.'

'FAM-LEE!' Boja cheered, quick to claim his place at the table.

And so, for the first time in a long time, all the Everdews ate together. Boja watched them using knives and forks, but couldn't do it himself without flinging slices of apple at Santoro, so he gave up and ate with his paws instead. Ventillo remarked what an excellent idea that was, and started using her hands too. Soon they were all gleefully shovelling duck eggs, buttered wildercakes and the occasional bit of apple into their mouths, before washing it all down with hot tea.

Dev remarked on the silver heart hanging around his

mother's neck, and she showed it off to everyone.

'Bastor made it for me,' she proudly said. 'Sorry, I should say, *Acting Mayor* Bastor. Works rather well as a necklace, don't you think?'

Dev replied that it did. Ventillo shrugged. Boja was staring wistfully at Santoro's plate, having long since emptied his own, and Santoro was trying to ignore him. But, eventually, he relented and slid what was left of his dinner in front of the hungry bear.

'Your brother invented something quite incredible.' Ventillo waved her fork at Santoro. 'Quite, quite miraculous. You finally saw it, didn't you?'

'It was . . . impressive.' Santoro quietly nodded.

'Impressive?' Amy smiled. 'When Boja lit up that tree like a firework? The sheer *power* of it. It was stunning!'

'*BWOOOOSCHHHH!*' Boja cheered through a mouthful of apple, raising his arms triumphantly in the air.

'It was nice to see you two finally working together,' Ventillo said, huddling closer to Santoro and sharing her shawl with him. That smile returned to his lips. He tried to stifle it, but Dev saw.

'I did what Dad would have done,' Santoro said.

'That you did.' Amy shuffled her chair up next to them, and beckoned for Dev to join in. 'And you were right, he'd have been proud of you. Both of you.'

There they sat for some time, bundled together, one big mass of Everdews. And then Boja could hold back no more. He stood up and wrapped his huge arms around them all, dragging them into his pillowy soft belly, before losing his balance and crashing through the table.

'FAM-LEE!' he cheered, rolling around on the floor.

The Everdews shrieked and giggled.

So he squidged them tighter.

'Family.' Dev smiled, curling up into the bear's fur like a baby in a rug.

An Ending

A Beginning

Dev's workshop was just how he'd left it; absolutely destroyed.

Moonlight spilled down through the open ceiling, glinting off all the smashed glass on the floor. The collapsed furniture cast long, ominous shadows across endless fluttering scraps of paper, reaching all the way towards the back of the workshop, or at least, where the back had once been. Now it was just a massive, gaping hole.

And an extraordinary view of the stars

Dev pulled a couple of oil lamps out from the rubble, lit and hung them from the drooping rafters. He swept away the worst of the glass. Cleared a space in the middle of the floor. Then he pulled Boja through the doorway – first an arm, then an eyeball, and finally his huge, lumpy body.

Once Boja was upright and had stopped fidgeting, Dev set to work.

He shone torches up Boja's nostrils, he stuck thermometers in his ears. He pulled on Boja's fingers, one by one, until finally one of them produced a squeak from Boja's bum. And then he pulled on it again, over and over, squeak after squeak, collapsing Boja into a giggling mess.

For over an hour he tested the big red bear. Seeing what Boja could do. Making notes. Endless notes. Trying to find something, anything, that could solve the problem that had been nagging at him all evening.

Bumblebuss had been right. The one person Dev hadn't wanted to be right. He was so right.

The Eden Tree needed its flember back.

But how to do it? Its flember was keeping Boja alive, and the idea of Boja sacrificing himself . . . well, it was unthinkable. Boja was now a living thing, just like everyone else.

A loud snore rattled out from Boja's nostrils. He had fallen asleep on his feet.

There would be no more testing tonight.

Dev, however, wasn't tired. He walked towards the missing half of his workshop and sat down on the edge of the floorboards, dangling his legs into the night air. He took a deep breath. Listened to the spindletrees swaying gently in the wind, the bindle-bugs chirping in the reeds.

And then, beneath his feet, he saw the distinct glow of flember.

'The book!'
Dev exclaimed as,
with the longest
stretch, he was
just able to haul
it up with his
fingertips. Once
safe, he held his
hand above the
cover, watching
as thin wisps of
flember danced
up from its golden
F and lapped
against his palm.

Dev read the book three more times that night. But he learnt nothing new, found no clues, no answers, and eventually his own eyes were too tired to focus on the words. He stretched, yawned and, clutching the book to his chest, turned around to go to bed.

Boja was standing behind him. No longer asleep, but quite, quite alert. In his paws he held a flower pot, or rather, *the* flower pot, the one from Dev's first experiment. And inside the flower pot, the white-drop. The beautiful, delicate whitedrop, as alive as it had ever been.

'Shared.' Boja beamed, his fingers sparkling with flember.

Dev smiled. 'Feels good, doesn't it?'

'*Smells* good.' Boja leant down and, before Dev could stop him, he took a great big sniff of the flower.

It disappeared, soil and all, up inside his nostril, his whole face contorting with the shock.

'AAA—'

'Boja, no!'

'—CHOOOOOOOOOO!'

Boja stumbled backwards, great globules of glowing blue snot flying scattershot across the walls. Instinctively, Dev opened the flember book up as a shield, and a huge sticky lump squelched against it.

He lowered the book back down. It had taken most of the blast, thankfully, but now both pages were soaked with snot. Dev grumbled. Cast Boja a frown.

And then he noticed the lines.

Right there, on the snot covered pages. Glowing out between the words. Lines travelling up, down and across the pages.

Dev's own heart started to pound faster.

'Boja, take the book.'

Boja resisted, unsure if he was in trouble or not.

'Fire it up. R-run flember through it. The whole

book.'

Still Boja hesitated.

'Boja, *SHARE.*' Dev thrust the book into his paws.

Instantly, sparks spun around Boja's fingertips and into the book, through the pages, lighting each one in a brilliant glow. More lines appeared, along with symbols; strange geometric symbols, carving up the lines, splitting them in all directions. And markers too, distances, a network of measurements, all sparkling as if written in starlight.

Dev gasped . . .

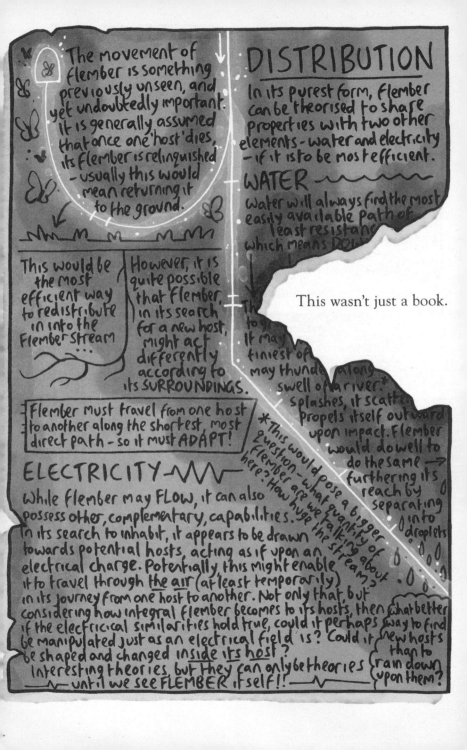

The movement of flember is something previously unseen, and yet undoubtedly important. It is generally assumed that once one 'host' dies, its flember is relinquished - usually this would mean returning it to the ground.

DISTRIBUTION

In its purest form, flember can be theorised to share properties with two other elements - water and electricity - if it is to be most efficient.

WATER

Water will always find the most easily available path of least resistance which means DOW...

This wasn't just a book.

This would be the most efficient way to redistribute in into the Flember stream ....

However, it is quite possible that Flember, in its search for a new host, might act differently according to its SURROUNDINGS.

Th... to g... It may... tiniest of... may thunder along swell of a river.* splashes, it scatter... propels itself outward upon impact. Flember would do well to do the same → furthering its reach by separating into droplets

Flember must travel from one host to another along the shortest, most direct path - so it must ADAPT!

*This would pose a bigger question - what quantity of flember are we talking about here? How huge the stream?

ELECTRICITY

While flember may FLOW, it can also possess other, complementary, capabilities. In its search to inhabit, it appears to be drawn towards potential hosts, acting as if upon an electrical charge. Potentially, this might enable it to travel through the air (at least temporarily) in its journey from one host to another. Not only that, but considering how integral flember becomes to its hosts, then what better if the electrical similarities hold true, could it perhaps sway to find be manipulated just as an electrical field is? Could it new hosts be shaped and changed inside its host? than to Interesting theories, but they can only be theories rain down until we see FLEMBER itself!! upon them?

It was a **map**.

Dev and Boja's adventures continue in

FLEMBER

BOOK 2

coming soon...

Acknowledgements

Some stories take a while to tell, and that is definitely true of *Flember*. Along the way a great many people have helped me – too many names to list, but I hope you know who you are, and how much I appreciate it.

A special thanks to Catherine for your help at the start of this journey.

And an extra special thanks to David and Rosie, for your endless patience, and your enduring faith in *Flember*.

FLEMBER
- SKETCHES -

HUFF!
PUFF!

BANG!

David Fickling Books

JAMIE SMART'S

BUNNY VS MONKEY

'One of the best children's comics of all time!'
Starburst Magazine

This is good vs evil. Science vs nature. This is
BUNNY VS MONKEY!

If you go down to the woods today, you're sure of
a big – MECHANICAL MOLE TANK?!
Wait, that doesn't sound right . . .
Prepare for chicken zeppelins,
the PIG-O-TRON 5000, the
indestructable Action Beaver, a
squirrel with a passion
for baking and loads more!

'Endlessly inventive, sublimely funny and outrageously addictive, Bunny vs Monkey is the kind of comic parents beg kids to read to them. Don't miss out on the next big thing.' *Now Read This!*

David Fickling Books

JAMIE SMART'S

You may think that your cat is crazy, but they've got nothing on Looshkin. Leave him for just a moment and you'll find that your house has flooded, a steam train has smashed into your living room and a portal to another dimension has opened in your loft. And everything is covered in bees. Looshkin, what have you done?!

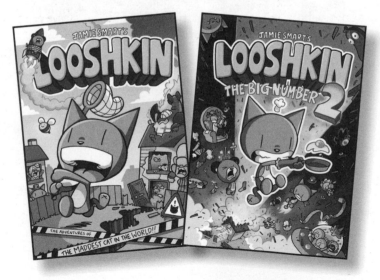

About Jamie

Jamie Smart has been creating children's comics for many years, with popular titles including *Bunny vs Monkey*, *Looshkin*, and *Fish-Head Steve* which became the first work of its sort to be shortlisted for the Roald Dahl Funny Prize. He also works on multimedia projects like Find Chaffy.

Jamie lives in the south-east of England, where he spends his time thinking up stories and getting lost on dog walks. This is his first novel.